# THE SHAPE-SHIFTER'S
# CURSE

Read the first book in
the Magic Repair Shop series:

**The Multiplying Menace**

# THE SHAPE-SHIFTER'S
# CURSE

## A Magic Repair Shop Book

Amanda Marrone

Aladdin

New York  London  Toronto  Sydney

This book is a work of fiction. Any references to historical events, real people, or real locales
are used fictitiously. Other names, characters, places, and incidents are the product of the author's imagination,
and any resemblance to actual events or locales or persons, living or dead, is entirely coincidental.

**ALADDIN**

An imprint of Simon & Schuster Children's Publishing Division

1230 Avenue of the Americas, New York, NY 10020

First Aladdin paperback edition November 2010

Copyright © 2010 by Amanda Marrone

All rights reserved, including the right of reproduction in whole or in part in any form.

ALADDIN is a trademark of Simon & Schuster, Inc., and related logo

is a registered trademark of Simon & Schuster, Inc.

For information about special discounts for bulk purchases, please contact Simon & Schuster Special Sales

at 1-866-506-1949 or business@simonandschuster.com.

The Simon & Schuster Speakers Bureau can bring authors to your live event. For more information

or to book an event contact the Simon & Schuster Speakers Bureau at 1-866-248-3049

or visit our website at www.simonspeakers.com.

Designed by Mike Rosamilia

The text of this book was set in Centaur MT.

Manufactured in the United States of America 0910 OFF

2 4 6 8 10 9 7 5 3 1

Library of Congress Control Number 2010905112

ISBN 978-1-4169-9034-5

ISBN 978-1-4391-5823-4 (eBook)

For my mother
and world traveler, Marilou Foley,
who would love to have a magic mirror
to go overseas at the drop of a hat.
We so need to go to Scotland.

Many thanks to my editor, Kate Angelella, for her patience and shiny stickers that make me feel like a rock star, and my agent, Wendy Schmalz for always believing in me. Thanks to Nina Nelson, Pam Foard, and Naomi Panzer for always supporting me and reading on the fly. As always, thanks to my husband, Joe, for listening to new plot developments even when he'd rather be watching football. Thanks to everyone at Aladdin for working so hard to make the repair shop a reality!

# 1

## Defying Gravity

As soon as Gram left the apartment Sunday morning to work at the food pantry, I raced to my room and slipped on my shoes. After everything that had happened in the last week, Gram had decided the magic repair shop was too dangerous and I was forbidden to go there. But I knew I couldn't stay away. I *had* to get Mr. McGuire to convince Gram to let me work there.

That's not to say I didn't understand why Gram didn't want me to go down to the shop anymore. I'd been in Connecticut for less than a week and already I'd already been attacked by a lion and kidnapped by a crazed magician, and just two nights ago I was seconds away from spending the rest of my life in a magic mirror.

Getting her to change her mind was going to be harder than teaching an elephant to ride a unicycle on a tightrope.

I grabbed my keys off my night table and bumped Hasenpfeffer's cage. Grimacing, I crossed my fingers and hoped I hadn't woken him up.

"For pity's sake," he snapped. He poked his furry white head out from under his blanket, blinking his pink eyes in the light. "Can't a rabbit take a nap in peace?"

"Sorry."

"You're always *sorry*, Maggie," he continued. "How about you just watch where those enormous feet of yours are going?"

"They're only a size four!"

Hasenpfeffer sat up on his haunches. "Yet they somehow *always* manage to hit my cage."

I rolled my eyes. There'd been more than one occasion I'd regretted casting the spell that gave him speech—even if it had been by accident—and this was one of them. "*Fine*, I'll move your cage away from my bed where I won't bang into it."

I looked around the tiny bedroom I'd be staying in for

the next year while my parents were hunting cockroaches in the Amazon. There weren't a lot of options. "How about over there, by the window?"

Hasenpfeffer peered at the window overlooking the street below. "What, and get heatstroke when the afternoon sun comes in? No thank you."

I pointed to the other side of the room by my closet.

He shook his head. "Too drafty."

"By the computer?"

"What, and listen to that infernal humming all the time? Tsk. There really isn't a good spot in this shoe box of a room." He chattered his teeth as he sniffed around, peering into every corner. "I'm not used to being in such confined quarters all the time. I miss the grand hotel rooms when Milo and I traveled; I miss performing and hearing the cheers as I got pulled out of the hat. Look what's become of me. Stuck here with nothing to do all day but stare at an overabundance of unicorn posters."

He sniffed, and I wondered if it was possible for a rabbit to cry.

"I never imagined I'd retire this early," he continued, "but I thought if I ever did, I'd be living it up in a spacious hutch in Japan. Milo and I were *very* popular in Japan. I even got fan mail." He let out a long, mournful sigh.

I decided not to remind him he was stuck with me

because his former owner, Milo the Magnificent, had *abandoned* him in the magic repair shop. The fact that Milo had tried to kill me apparently had no effect on Hasenpfeffer's longing for his old life.

"Well, I'm going for a walk," I said, trying to sound light and breezy. "Tell Gram if she gets home before I do, okay?"

"Oh, please. You're going to the shop. And don't pretend otherwise." He shook his head. "You're a terrible actress."

"I'm not going to the shop!" I lied. "I'm just going for a walk. You know—fresh air, sunshine."

"I demand parsley or I tell the old woman you're with McGuire."

"That's blackmail," I said, putting my hands on my hips.

He put a paw on his nearly empty food dish. "Call it what you want, but it would be *very* easy to forget this conversation ever happened if I had a belly full of parsley."

I squeezed my eyes shut tight. "Fine, you win."

"Make it the flat-leaf *Italian* parsley. It's my favorite and easier on my digestive system."

I shook my head as I took out my grandfather's old wooden wand—curved and bent like a tree branch—from my desk drawer. After working out a simple rhyme in my head, I pointed the wand at Hasenpfeffer's cage. *"Garden's growing rather sparsely, let's just get a crop of parsley."* A shower of green sparks shot from the tip, and then Hasenpfeffer's bowl filled to the top with parsley.

He hopped over and sniffed. "Ah. Perfect." He grabbed a mouthful and started chewing noisily. "Tell McGuire I said hello," he mumbled.

I walked down the steps to the sidewalk and looked up at the apartment above mine, where Raphael lived. I would've asked him to come with me, but I knew he was at his bagpipe lessons.

I shook my head. Who takes *bagpipe* lessons?

Since Raphael was a twelve-year-old genius, I was sure he could help me to think up the perfect argument to convince Gram that working in the shop was safe; but in the meantime, Mr. McGuire and I would be on our own.

I headed down a couple of blocks and finally turned at the corner of Barnum Avenue, where McGuire and Malloy's Magic Repair Shop was located. A beat-up blue van covered with large daisy decals was parked out front. When I got closer I saw a magnetic sign on the van that read CLARENCE'S MAGICAL CLOWNING.

I wrinkled my nose. I had never much cared for clowns.

I walked down the steps to the basement storefront and slowly opened the door.

My eyes popped when I stepped inside. An orange rabbit with purple paws and ears was turning slowly in the air. Birthday hats, a deflated green balloon, a partially eaten hamburger, and several brightly colored, wrapped presents orbited the rabbit like disorderly planets around a sun. The rabbit seemed unconcerned as it drifted in lazy circles, and I couldn't help smiling thinking about what Hasenpfeffer would say if he were in this situation. He wouldn't be taking it so calmly, that's for sure.

"Maggie!" Mr. McGuire said. "What are you doing here? I thought your grandmother made it clear you weren't to come down again."

I turned and saw Mr. McGuire standing next to a small man who looked like he could be a hundred years old. He was bone thin and dressed in a baggy orange clown suit. His white makeup gathered in the deep creases on his face, and the blue diamonds painted around his eyes glistened with tears. As he tugged on the oversize pink bowtie under his chin and pointed to the rabbit, I couldn't help thinking this clown was looking sad not scary.

"Are you Maggie?" the man asked, squinting at me. "Gregory said he was wishing you was here to help. It's my Gertrude who needs fixin.'" He pointed to the rabbit again. "She's been like that for three hours now. I can't lose her; she's all I got—well except for the wife, but Gertrude is the only one who really understands me."

"I just came to talk about . . ." I paused, unable to keep my eyes off the gravity-defying rabbit.

Mr. McGuire snapped his suspenders. "Maggie Malloy, meet Mr. Clarence Fishbone. He had a bit of a mishap at a birthday party earlier today."

The old man scowled. "There were nearly twenty of them—*twenty rotten kids*. They laughed at me, they did. Didn't think I could do nuttin. They know better now."

"What happened?" I asked.

Mr. Fishbone shook his head mournfully. "The wife keeps telling me I'm too old for putting on shows, but we've gots bills to pay. So I take the job for this Billy kid's fifth birthday, and as soon as I walked in I knew it was gonna be trouble. Them kids was pawing through me stuff—they let the pigeons loose and one of 'em dumped a whole jar of magic dust number seven into me hat."

I looked at Mr. McGuire. "A whole jar?"

"A whole jar," he echoed.

Mr. McGuire had told me that a *teaspoon* of magic dust number seven gave extra power to spells, so it was easy to understand why he was having difficulty repairing this particular one.

Mr. Fishbone took the daisy-covered, dome-shaped hat off his head and brought it to his chest. His faded brown eyes misted over as he clutched it tightly. "Me grand finale is something special. I don't just *pull* a rabbit out of me hat like most party magicians do—I have Gertrude *float* out." He raised the hat slowly in the air to mimic the effect.

"Showstopper it is, I tell you. Only when Gertrude floated out today, she started *attracting* things. Hats got ripped of kids' heads. Presents floated up, and well, as you can guess, that wasn't real popular with Billy. Had a bit of tantrum he did. But the worst part was my poor Gertrude floating like a balloon on the ceiling and me not being able to do anything about it. Luckily, Gregory here was on call and able to cast a containment spell around her so she wouldn't float off."

His face crumpled as he looked at Gertrude hovering just out of reach.

"What have you tried so far?" I asked Mr. McGuire.

"I haven't been at it long, but the various rabbit-in-the-hat spells didn't work."

I turned to Mr. Fishbone. "What spell did you use to make Gertrude levitate?"

He scratched the purple wig on his head. "I've got it written down somewhere. The wife insists I write everything down now. She wasn't happy when I made the laundry disappear and couldn't remember which spell I'd used. Had to go buy new underwear we did."

He reached into a giant pocket and pulled out a handful of what looked like glowing jelly beans. "That's not it." He walked over to a lime green, daisy-covered suitcase on the floor and opened it. He rifled inside a bit, tossing colored scarves and oversize playing cards on the floor, before coming up with a worn piece of paper.

"Here it is!" He squinted at it, and then held it at arm's length. *"In the hat my Gertrude lies, but like the sun, she'll start to rise."*

The spell seemed ordinary enough, and I figured it was definitely the magic dust number seven that had twisted the trick. The question now was how to repair it.

I tilted my head as I watched Gertrude float. My mind raced and clicked until I realized the scene reminded me of video clips I'd seen of astronauts floating in zero gravity.

"How about a gravity spell?" I asked Mr. McGuire.

Mr. McGuire's eyes lit up. "Of course! I have a book that addresses gravitational problems in the back room. I'll just be a minute to find it."

He pushed aside the curtains that hung in the doorway separating the back room from the main shop.

With my eyes I followed the trajectories of the objects orbiting Gertrude and hoped we could fix this spell quickly. Mr. McGuire and I needed to strategize before Gram got back from work.

"Hang in there, Gertrude," Clarence said. "These people will get you back to normal."

"Have you always been a stage magician?" I asked him, curious about why some magicians perform and others don't.

He shook his head and removed the red foam ball from his nose. "Oh, I'm not a stage magician—I don't have me the power to pull off all that fancy stuff. It's just parties I do. It's different now, though. Kids want more." He sighed. "I could blow the socks off them kiddies, I know I could. If only . . ." He gave me a sly smile as his eyes sparkled. "Well, I can show *you*."

He went back over to his suitcase and pulled out a long red balloon and an air pump. He quickly inflated the balloon and twisted it with surprisingly nimble fingers. When he was done, he placed a shiny balloon dachshund on the floor and took a yellow wand out of his oversize pocket. *"Inflate, animate, sit, and stay, dogs will bark, dogs will obey."*

Mr. Fishbone beamed as the dog sat on its rubber bottom and opened its latex mouth to let out a series of high-pitched yips and yaps that echoed around the room. He waved his wand in tight circles, and the dog rolled over and over. He lifted the wand straight in the air and the dog stood up and danced on its little hind legs. It howled at the ceiling, and Mr. Fishbone flicked his wand, returning the balloon dog to its original, nonmagical state.

"Wow." I laughed. "That *would* blow the socks off the kids. You'd be booked for months in advance." But as the words left my mouth I knew that wasn't possible. "Except . . ."

Mr. Fishbone nodded sadly. "It would be obvious it was real magic and not sleight of hand—and definitely not a Viola Klemp–approved trick. She thinks it's best people don't know magic is real. I suppose she's right. Don't think she'd be real happy if she knew about Gertrude's levitating trick, but I always tell the kids I does it with mirrors."

Viola Klemp was the head of the Society for Ethical Magicians. Years ago she'd been sawed in half by a stage magician who didn't have the power to pull the trick off properly. After Mr. McGuire and my grandfather had finally found a spell to put her two halves back together—*four days later*—she'd started the society as a way to keep track of magicians behaving badly.

I grimaced. I was currently under investigation by

Viola thanks to my fellow magician and classmate Darcy Davenport. I shook my head to chase the thought away. "Don't worry about Gertrude. We'll get her fixed up."

Mr. Fishbone smiled. "The wife used to help out with me act, but she got tired of dressing up—said she was too old for feathers and sequins. She used to look real cute too, but now it's just Gertrude and me. It's real nice Gregory has an assistant like you to help out, someone to pass the business on to and such."

I sighed. Unless we changed Gram's mind, my apprenticeship in the shop was officially over. As it was, Gram would kill me if she knew I was here.

Mr. McGuire came out from the back room and placed a large, leather-bound book with yellowed pages on the wooden counter.

"*Defying Gravity and other Spells* by Sir Isaac Newton," I said, surprised. "*He* was a magician?"

"Oh yes," Mr. McGuire said. "It's rumored he was a poor student and used magic to get into the University of Cambridge."

My cheeks burned. I was pretty sure Mr. McGuire suspected I'd used magic to get into the Black Rock School for the Gifted and Talented—and he was right. But there was no way I could've passed the entrance exam if I hadn't. "So where's the spell?" I said, changing the subject.

He opened the book and ran a finger down the table of contents. "Page sixty." He flipped to the page, and I leaned over to look at the ingredients we'd need.

"'Restoring gravity,'" I read out loud. "'Half a cup of Origins powder.'" We'd used that before—it was made of stardust and helped get things back to their original states.

Mr. McGuire looked at Gertrude and clucked his tongue. "Better double that—just in case."

He'd told me how expensive Origins powder was, and I wondered if Mr. Fishbone would be able to pay for this repair job. "'Two teaspoons of magic dust number four,'" I continued. "That helps bind the ingredients," I said to Mr. Fishbone.

Mr. McGuire smiled at me like he was proud I'd remembered what it was used for. Instead of feeling happy, I thought about how this most likely would be the last time I'd get to repair something, and my heart sank.

"'Two cups of pulverized granite,'" I continued.

Mr. McGuire's eyes lit up. "To add weight to the spell—help get her down." He rubbed his hands gleefully. "I haven't pulverized rocks in such a long time."

"Oh! Can I help?" Mr. Fishbone asked as he shook his fists excitedly at his sides.

Mr. McGuire hustled to the back room. "I'll get us some goggles!"

I looked down at the book again and shook my head. "The last ingredients are three slices of dehydrated apple and gunpowder." I looked quizzically at Mr. McGuire when he returned. "Gunpowder?"

"What goes up must come down," Mr. McGuire said, pointing to the ceiling. "The gunpowder will send the spell up to Gertrude, and then down she'll come."

"She won't get hurt?" Mr. Fishbone asked, worry filling his eyes.

"No," Mr. McGuire said gently. "She'll be fine—if Maggie's a good catch."

"I used to play softball—outfield," I said, and Mr. Fishbone look relieved.

Mr. McGuire and Mr. Fishbone took turns blowing up chunks of granite with their wands. Every time a rock got zapped, it let off a loud pop and exploded into a fine powder, making them chuckle and hoot like schoolboys.

When they were done, I added the rock powder to the mixing bowl and used my wand to magically stir the ingredients. Mr. McGuire took the bowl and placed it under Gertrude and her collection of party-themed satellites. "Ready?" he asked.

I nodded and knelt on the floor, positioning myself underneath her with my hands held open.

Mr. McGuire pointed his wand at the bowl. *"Newton's apple needs to drop, ignite the spark to hit the mark."*

A mini–lightning bolt zigzagged out of his wand and hit the bowl. Blue and orange flames shot up straight in the air, and I leaned back, gasping.

"Gertrude!" Mr. Fishbone wailed.

I suddenly realized the flames weren't producing any heat, but as the tips reached the hovering objects, they dropped like stones toward the floor. I dove and caught Gertrude in my arms just as the hamburger landed on my head. A pickle bounced out from under the bun and rolled down my forehead and nose, leaving a trail of ketchup in its wake.

"Ew," I said as Mr. Fishbone scooped Gertrude out of my arms.

"Baby," he cooed. "It's all right now, everything's fine."

He snuggled and kissed his rabbit, and it reminded me of Raphael talking to his pet mouse, Pip. I wondered if I'd ever feel that way about Hasenpfeffer—not that I imagined he'd ever want to be kissed!

Mr. Fishbone turned to Mr. McGuire, nervousness replacing the relief in his eyes. "Gregory, I don't know how to thank you, but . . ." He hugged Gertrude tight.

"Things is kinda tight at home right now, and I don't think I'm getting paid for Billy's party and all." He looked at the floor and shuffled his large clown shoes. "Do you think maybe you could fix me up with one of them payment plans? I'll try to find me some more work, and I'll make sure you get your money just as *soon* as I can."

Mr. McGuire shook his head. "It's on the house, Clarence. Don't give it another thought."

Mr. Fishbone looked down again, embarrassed. "Thank you," he said in a whisper. "Thank you." He jostled his rabbit in his arms and kissed her on the top of her head. "I best be going; get Gertrude settled in her hutch and give her a nice treat for all she's been through."

"Good to see you, Clarence," Mr. McGuire said as he patted him gently on the back. "Give Celeste my love."

"I will." He gathered up his things and cradled Gertrude gently in his arms. "And it's been very nice to meet you, Maggie. Thanks to you both. I'll keep you in me prayers."

I watched him walk up the stairs to the sidewalk with a happy bounce in his old legs, and all I could think was that repairing magic was *way* better than being some stupid stage magician like Milo—or even a magical clown like Clarence.

What would I do if Gram didn't change her mind?

"Maggie," Mr. McGuire said gently after Mr. Fishbone's van drove off. "You really shouldn't be here. Your grandmother made it quite clear how she felt about you continuing to work here. And after what happened, I can't say I blame her."

Tears pricked my eyes. "But Milo's gone—he's trapped in the mirror. Things are safe now—just tell her. She'll listen to you. She has to."

Suddenly a loud rattling noise caught our attention. We both turned toward the noise, and I saw a silver mailbox nailed on the wall behind the counter jumping around on its hook. Steam shot out from the door, which was slightly ajar, and it began to whistle like a teakettle. The letters VK glowed and wavered in the mist.

"Oh dear," Mr. McGuire said, putting a hand to his lip. "Mail's coming—from Viola Klemp."

My stomached did a slow somersault. "About me?"

He nodded slightly. "I'm sure it's nothing to worry about."

But from his pursed lips and wrinkled brow, I knew he was lying.

## Viola's Decree

Mr. McGuire ran his hands up and down his suspenders a few times. "Well, let's see what Viola has to say," he said, trying to sound cheerful as he walked over to the mailbox.

He waved away the steam before opening the door and taking out an envelope made of stiff, brown parchment. He held it up, and I could see the initials VK stamped in hardened bloodred wax on the back. He clucked his tongue as he took a letter opener from under the counter and slipped it along the top edge. "Viola's a bit old-fashioned," he said. "Even I don't use sealing wax anymore."

I held my breath as he took the letter out and pushed his glasses up the bridge of his nose. He shook his head and clucked his tongue some more as his eyes traced the letter.

"Well?" I asked, ready to burst.

He looked up from the paper and sighed. "It seems the Davenports *have* requested an investigation." He cleared his throat. "'I, Viola Klemp, using the authority granted to me by the Society of Ethical Magicians, decree there is enough evidence to support an investigation into the conduct of one Maggie Malloy, aged twelve, residing at seventy-seven Barn Swallow Boulevard, Apartment 107, Bridgeport, Connecticut. I will examine the statements of one Delilah Davenport and her daughter, Darcy, and will be in touch with my findings and recommendations after consulting with the chairperson of the Federation of Magic. Best wishes—'"

"Who's making wishes?" Raphael said as he pushed through the door carrying a plastic cage. "Not Maggie, I hope."

"Raphael!" I said in surprise.

He walked over to the counter and placed the cage on it. Pip was inside racing along in a tiny wheel as if there were a hungry cat hot on her tail. My eyes drifted around the shop until I spotted Olaf, a lemon yellow cat who Mr. McGuire was taking care. Olaf was curled up on a shelf between a container of porcupine quills and a jar of vampire teeth. The old cat eyed Pip, then yawned and closed his eyes as if deciding a mouse in a cage wasn't worth any bother.

Raphael hopped onto a stool behind the counter, sat up straight, and folded his hands neatly in front of him. "So what's on the agenda today? Mending broken wands, de-hexing curses, or vanquishing more evil magicians? Actually, I haven't been able to find any data about the chances of surviving an encounter with a deadly magician, but Milo was more than enough, and I'd rather not press my luck if it's all the same to you."

"I'd like to vanquish a certain *pint-size* magician," I said, walking over to the counter. "We just got a letter from Viola Klemp; Darcy's mother *is* having me investigated."

Raphael turned to Mr. McGuire. "Is using magic to get into a private school and casting a few dozen spells to keep up with the work really *that* bad? I mean, compared to what Milo did—what with duplicating himself and stealing powers, not to mention murder—Maggie's wishes seem like small potatoes. Besides, the Davenports don't know the really bad stuff Maggie did, like—"

"Raphael!" I said through gritted teeth. "I don't think we need to mention each and every little spell I may or may not have cast."

I flushed as I caught Mr. McGuire eyeing me suspiciously. He knew I'd used magic to influence Gram to let me work in the shop in the first place, but I didn't want him to find out I'd used the same trick on Raphael. And I *especially* didn't want him to find out I'd also hit my parents with a *major* mind spell so they'd forget a crazed monkey I'd accidentally conjured up with wish magic on my fifth birthday.

Mr. McGuire folded his arms across his chest and looked at me with one eyebrow cocked. "Is there anything I should know before Viola interviews me about your conduct?"

"No, I'm good," I said nervously, "but Raphael is right. Is what I did really *that bad* compared to what some magicians are doing?"

"No," Mr. McGuire said, "but the Davenports are very influential in the magic community, and I'm guessing they've put a lot of pressure on Viola. Viola is also a stickler for ethical magic and perhaps she feels publicly investigating you sends a warning to other young magicians who might be tempted to use their magic to get ahead."

"But I didn't know about any of these rules when I made those wishes. Doesn't that count for something?

"Of course," Mr. McGuire said. "And I'm confident you'll walk out of this with a simple warning."

He smiled at me, but it didn't do anything to calm my fears. Darcy Davenport liked to be number one in everything she did, and if she thought I was a threat, there was no telling how far she'd go to stay on top.

"Uh-oh," Raphael said. "What if Viola Klemp asks *me* to vouch for your character and she uses magic to prevent me from lying? My testimony would sink your case."

I glared at Raphael. "As always, your support is *underwhelming*."

"Let's not worry about Viola until we get her final report," Mr. McGuire said. "More important, I'd like to know where people think the two of you are."

"My mother is under the mistaken impression that I'm at Maggie's apartment," Raphael said.

Mr. McGuire shook his head and sighed.

"In all fairness," he continued, "I did call to see if Maggie was home, but Hasenpfeffer told me she had come down here."

"What?" I said. "*Hasenpfeffer* told you?"

Raphael nodded. "He was mad the ringing woke him up from a nap—apparently he's figured out how to push the talk button on the phone with his paw. He yelled at me for bothering him and said something about rabbits needing their beauty sleep and that I'd spoiled some great dream he was having about drinking clover tea in Japan."

"I just hope Gram doesn't call," I groaned. "She'll kill him—and me—if she finds out he's using the phone."

"Speaking of your grandmother," Mr. McGuire said, turning to me. "I expect she'd be surprised to discover you're here as well."

I forced a big smile on my face. "Kind of. She's at the food pantry; she thinks I'm in my room studying the periodic table of elements for school. Funny, huh?"

Mr. McGuire shook his head. "Not funny. And you wouldn't think so either had you been on the receiving end of an hour-long tirade from your grandmother about how woefully inadequate I am at looking after children."

"Actually," I said, "I heard all about it when I was on the receiving end of my own 'tirade,' but you told Raphael and me to stay in my apartment when you went after Milo. It's not *your* fault we didn't listen."

"Hey," Raphael said, "I tried to get Maggie to stay put and call for help."

"But you went along with her anyway," Mr. McGuire said.

Raphael blushed. "She's really very persuasive," he said quietly.

Mr. McGuire nodded. "All the more reason you two should head home. If you're not here, there won't be any trouble to get into."

"But Milo's *gone*," I insisted. "And besides, how much trouble did you have in the shop before he showed up?"

Mr. McGuire scratched his balding head. "Actually, besides the magically induced flea outbreak of 1984, there hadn't been any major problems since the late seventies."

"See!" I said. "Milo was one of those . . . you know . . ."

"Flukes," Raphael finished for me. "A statistical anomaly!"

I nodded my head vigorously. "And how could Gram blame *you* for the trouble I got into just because Milo happened to show up in Bridgeport around the same time I did? None of us knew how dangerous he was."

"That's true," Mr. McGuire said. He pursed his lips. "Really, things had been rather dull for quite some time." His eyes twinkled, and I knew he wanted me working in the shop as much as I did. "Perhaps you're right. I could try to speak to your grandmother again. And what are the chances another magician like Milo will come along?"

Raphael cocked his head. "I'd say a trillion to one."

"And weren't you going to try to repair the mirror today?" I said. "That sounds like a *really* big job. You know, one that needs the help of a trusty assistant—or two."

"Hold on a minute," Raphael said as he hopped off

the stool and came around the counter. "You're really going to try and *fix* that mirror? The one with Milo in it? Isn't that just asking for the statistics to lean toward a reappearance of Bridgeport's public enemy number one?"

"No worries, Raphael," Mr. McGuire said. "My good friend Sir Roderick Lachlan—who just happens to be the chairperson of the World Federation of Magic—has the only other mirror in the world like mine. He's very well read on the workings of the mirror, and he assured me Milo isn't getting out on his own. The mirror is really a very useful tool in repairing magic, so it's imperative to my business that it gets repaired."

"I'm sorry I broke it," I said, apologizing for the millionth time.

"What better place to break something than a repair shop?" Mr. McGuire said with a wink.

"So what do we do?" I asked, pushing up my sleeves.

Mr. McGuire went to the back room and rolled out the mirror—or what was left of it. Only the frame and the caster wheels remained. He placed the blue fabric cover in a messy heap on the counter.

Raphael looked up and down at the empty frame. "Are you going to magic new glass?"

Mr. McGuire shook his head. "Ordinary glass won't do. The mirror's glass was enchanted hundreds of years ago in China by a very powerful sorceress who took the spell to her grave, so we'll have to reassemble it."

"Sorceress?" I asked.

"A sorceress is a conjuror of the greatest power," Mr. McGuire began, "one who is able to perform feats of magic far beyond the capabilities of ordinary magicians."

"So I guess there aren't too many people trying to make a mirror like this one?" I asked.

"Oh, there are those who have tried," Mr. McGuire said. "At least twenty people have been documented attempting to create similar mirrors—and all of them disappeared, never to be heard from again. Mirrors can be tricky to work with, and the inexperienced magician can mistakenly open portals to other worlds and end up much like Milo—trapped."

Raphael whistled. "Did I ever tell you guys how happy I am *not* to be a magician?"

"Yes," I said. "Almost as often as Hasenpfeffer reminds me he used to be in show business."

Mr. McGuire picked up a cardboard box from the floor. "Do you like jigsaw puzzles?"

Raphael's eyes lit up as he brushed his brown curls from his eyes. "I am t*he* jigsaw puzzle champion at our school. Last year I completed a one-thousand-piece puzzle in thirty-three point seven minutes, and I didn't even use the picture. I bested the runner-up, Serena Gupta, by half an hour."

Mr. McGuire looked my way.

"The last one I attempted was a ten-piece purple-pony puzzle in kindergarten, and I don't think I actually finished it."

"Well," Mr. McGuire said, "it's a good thing Raphael is here to help." He tilted the box and gently shook out shards of silver-coated glass that clinked and clanked like wind chimes as they spilled out.

Raphael whistled again. "I *told* Maggie breaking the mirror was a bad idea."

I shot him a look before turning to Mr. McGuire. "Don't tell me we have to put all those pieces back together by hand," I said, gaping at the pile. "Can't we use a spell?"

"No," Mr. McGuire said gravely. "If *any* magic other than the restoring spell is used on the glass, the shards will swarm up and imbed themselves into whoever tried the magic. Apparently the inventor didn't want her creation to outlive her."

I looked at the hundreds of sharp points glinting under the shop's fluorescent lights and gulped. "By hand it is, then."

While Raphael and I got to work carefully arranging

the pieces of glass into place, Mr. McGuire mixed the ingredients needed to reassemble the shards into a solid surface and reactivate the mirror.

When he was done, he added dozens of crushed four-leaf clovers into the bowl to cancel out my seven years of bad luck. Apparently that old wives' tale about breaking mirrors was true, which would explain why my shoelaces kept mysteriously untying themselves, causing me to trip no less than six times today. Couple that with all the bad luck I'd attracted in the last few days, and I encouraged him to add as many as possible.

An hour and a half later we—well, mostly Raphael—had placed almost all of the glass into a four-by-six foot rectangle on the floor. Our fingertips were scratched and cut, but Mr. McGuire fixed those up with a simple healing spell.

"Only one piece left," I said, staring at the round, dinner-plate-size hole toward the top of our reconstruction. The missing piece was the one Milo the Magnificent had been accidentally trapped in. I shivered and squeezed my eyes shut for a second to erase the image of Milo screaming at us from within the glass as he tried to pound and claw his way out two nights ago.

Mr. McGuire went behind the counter and brought out the chunk, wrapped in a piece of blue fabric that I'd torn from the cover. He unwrapped it and laid it in the empty hole, completing the "puzzle."

"There," he said, walking back over to the counter. "I'll sew this swatch of fabric back into the cover, and then we'll finish the job. He spread the cloth out and took his wand from his back pocket. *"With nimble hands I bewitch this, sew it up with many stitches."*

A spark of white light leapt from the tip of his wand, and then a thick, white thread snaked up through the fabric, hovering at attention. He dipped and lifted his wand, and the thread wove in and out of the fabric, sewing the piece neatly back into place. He gave the wand a sharp flick, and then the thread knotted itself and disappeared from sight; finishing the task so well it was impossible to see where the repair job had been.

"Wow," I said. "I wish we could've done something this simple with the glass!"

*"Maggie!"* Mr. McGuire cried.

Startled, I took a sharp intake of breath and stared at his pale face. "What?" I just . . ." Then I knew. I'd said the word "wish." I'd used *magic* on the shards of glass. Mr. McGuire's earlier warning echoed in my head.

We all turned and look down at the glass with wide eyes. My legs trembled and my heart thudded in my chest as the pieces started to vibrate on the floor.

"*Run, Maggie!*" Mr. McGuire screamed. "Out of the shop—now!"

But it was too late. The shards of glass zipped straight up into the air and darted around with a deafening clank of glass, like a swarm of angry bees.

"Maggie, go!" Raphael hollered. "Hurry!"

I gaped at the glass heading my way and knew I didn't have time to make it out of the shop. I focused on the back room. "*I wish I was there!*" I screamed, pointing toward the doorway.

I felt my body ripped from where I was standing, and in a dizzying second, I reappeared in the back room. Disorientated and nauseous, I stumbled, trying to keep my balance.

"Watch out!" Raphael yelled.

I blinked and saw the clattering shards change direction and fly full force toward me. "I, uh, I . . ." I stuttered, unable to get any words out.

Mr. McGuire raced to the counter as I threw myself to the floor, covered my head with my arms, and braced for the impact.

"*Narcissus loved with great affection, but let me cast a new reflection!*" Mr. McGuire called out.

Instead of hundreds of pieces of glass cutting into my skin, I felt like someone had just kicked sand at me.

I peeked between my fingers and saw the pointed slivers of glass quivering in midair a millimeter from my face and realized Mr. McGuire had cast the spell in the nick of time. In the blink of an eye, the pieces flew toward the mirror frame and reassembled themselves into a solid sheet of glass. An angry wind roared out of the mirror, and then swooped back in, and I could feel myself being pulled toward the glass.

"Raphael," Mr. McGuire shouted. "Help me with the cover before we get sucked in!"

The two of them hurried to the counter, picked up the blue cover, and quickly draped it over the mirror.

The wind died, and I let out a long breath as I sat up on my knees. "How did you know the spell would work with the glass flying everywhere?"

Mr. McGuire mopped his forehead with his red bandanna. "I didn't."

Suddenly the door flew open and Gram—red-faced and eyes blazing—stormed in. *"Maggie Malloy, what on earth are you doing here in this shop?"*

# 3

# Have Mirror;
# Will Travel

I lay on my bed staring at the ceiling. "You just *had* to answer the phone. Now I'll be grounded until my parents get back from the Amazon!"

"How was I to know it was your grandmother?" Hasenpfeffer asked from his cage. "Or that she'd ask to talk to you," he added.

I rolled over on my stomach and stared at Hasenpfeffer. "You couldn't have said I was in the shower or something?"

"I panicked," he said. "But I still don't think I should be *locked* in my cage just because *you* got caught. What kind of justice is that?"

The phone rang. "Aren't you going to get that?" I asked him sarcastically.

Hasenpfeffer chattered his teeth. "I fail to find that amusing since you've imprisoned me in this minuscule cage that's not even fit to house a gerbil."

"I spent almost a hundred dollars of my own money to have the pet store special order the largest rabbit cage available. They don't get any bigger than this!"

There was a knock on my door, and I sat up on the bed. "Come in," I said, hoping Gram wasn't going to yell at me again.

Gram opened the door and frowned. "Get your shoes on; we're going back to the shop."

I sat up even straighter. "What?" Gram had spent the last hour lecturing me about responsibility and broken trust. She'd also said that if I wanted to repair magic when I was eighteen, that was my business, but in the meantime I was never again to set foot on Barnum Avenue, let alone go to the shop.

"Apparently Gregory has some news that can't be shared on the phone, but just because I'm taking you down there, don't think I've changed my mind about you working there."

I nodded, but after I got my shoes on I double crossed my fingers and hoped Mr. McGuire had a plan.

As Gram and I walked down the block to the magic repair shop in silence, I tried to think of something to say that might get her out of the black mood she was in so she'd be more receptive to un-grounding me.

"Um," I began as I juggled Hasenpfeffer in my arms. "We were able to repair the mirror I broke. No more seven years of bad luck for me." I tried to laugh, but it came out more like a high-pitched wheeze.

Gram scoffed. "Well, that's a relief. Heaven knows the world needs *more* magic mirrors to trap innocent young girls in."

"Ha!" Hasenpfeffer said. "Good one, Granny."

"I'm *not* your granny!" Gram snapped. "Why you let that rabbit continue to talk is beyond me," she added.

"Good question," I said, giving Hasenpfeffer a look.

Hasenpfeffer stared up at me, horror-struck. "What? You'd be lost without me. And who else would've pointed out that you had an embarrassing amount of unicorn posters hanging on your walls?"

"Some people like unicorns," I muttered. The sad thing was, I'd actually taken a couple down to shut him up.

"Oh, please," Hasenpfeffer said. "*Pink* unicorns? It's unnatural!"

I glared at him. "So are talking rabbits!"

We rounded the corner and I saw the small neon MCGUIRE AND MALLOY'S MAGIC REPAIR SHOP sign glowing above the stairs leading down to the basement store-front.

Suddenly a huge boom rattled the windows of the mostly abandoned apartments on the block.

"Save me!" Hasenpfeffer wailed, as he hid his head under my arm. "I used to be in show business; I'm more important than you people."

My eyes popped as clouds of pink smoke erupted from the small basement window of the repair shop. The door flew open, and Mr. McGuire staggered up the steps to the sidewalk coughing and wiping his eyes with a red bandanna.

"Gregory!" Gram shrieked as we ran to his side. "Are you all right?"

He fanned away the pink smoke with a piece of paper that was burnt around the bottom edges. "I'm fine, I'm fine!" He coughed into the bandanna, and then held the paper at arm's length, squinting. "I could have sworn that last ingredient was an orange slice, but when I dropped it in the cauldron, the whole thing exploded."

Gram held out her hand, and he gave her the smoldering paper. She gave the list a once-over and then shot him a withering look.

"Gregory, it clearly says 'ogre lice' and if *this*"—she waved at the smoke—"doesn't show you it's time to pack it in, what will? You could've been killed. Thank heavens Maggie wasn't down there."

Mr. McGuire's cheeks flushed. "It's just that I couldn't find my glasses, and I misread the last ingredient."

I pointed to the glasses perched in his sparse gray hair. "They're up there." This wasn't the first time he'd "lost" his glasses on the top of his head.

Mr. McGuire reached up and felt around for them. "So they are." He put the glasses on the bridge of his nose and then took the list back from Gram. "Yes, of course—ogre lice. It makes perfect sense. I'm whipping up a batch of stain remover. I had a little trouble with some dragon's blood," he said, pointing to a vivid green blotch on his shirt. "A crushed ogre louse is just the thing for tough stains. If only the detergent companies knew how well those little buggers foam up, they'd revolutionize the industry."

He looked up from his shirt and gave a start.

Gram was tapping her foot impatiently on the sidewalk and giving him the evil eye. "Is *this* why you insisted we had to come immediately? To extol the virtues of *ogre lice*?"

Mr. McGuire shook his head. "No! I mean, I *could* go

on about the many uses of ogre lice, but I have the most wonderful news for Maggie." He glanced at his watch and then cocked his head toward the shop. "Let's head down. I think you'll be excited to hear about an amazing opportunity that's come up."

"I guess it's too much to hope you're announcing your retirement," Gram said.

Mr. McGuire clucked his tongue. "Oh, this is much better than that. Maggie's going to Scotland for her World Federation of Magic testing!"

Scotland? Really?" I put Hasenpfeffer on the floor of the shop and blew away some of the pink smoke hovering in the air. Mr. McGuire had told me about the test, which would pinpoint the extent of my magical abilities, but I'd never dreamed it would happen in a foreign country.

Hasenpfeffer let out a long, dramatic cough. "Can't breath. Someone perform mouth-to-mouth if I lose consciousness." He rolled on his side and panted, but not without taking a quick peek to see if he'd gotten our attention.

"Let me clean this up," Mr. McGuire said. "Then we can talk."

He took a wand out of his back pants pocket and

pointed the tip at the wisps of pinkish clouds drifting up from a small cauldron on the large wooden counter. *"A mixed-up ingredient, but do not despair. What we need is a breath of fresh air."* He walked around the shop holding out his wand, and the lingering smoke was sucked into the tip like it was a vacuum.

Hasenpfeffer inhaled deeply. "Ah, that's better," he said, sitting up on his haunches. "So when do we leave for Scotland? I used to be a world traveler, you know."

I rolled my eyes. "We *know.*"

He twitched his nose as he looked around the shop's cluttered shelves full of books, canisters of magical powders, and an odd assortment of things like jellyfish tentacles and harpy feathers. "I am *really* looking forward to a change of scenery. This shop is dreary with a capital *D!*"

"What is this nonsense all about, Gregory?" Gram asked.

Mr. McGuire walked over to the mirror and straightened the blue cover embroidered with intricate stars and swirls.

"Brace yourselves," he said as he rested a hand on top of the mirror. *"Sir Roderick Lachlan* has agreed to perform Maggie's official magical-abilities test at his castle on the Orkney Islands in Scotland. I've made all of the arrangements. Maggie will leave Friday evening, and she'll be back Sunday, so there are no worries about missing school."

"Sir Roderick Lachlan?" I asked. "Didn't you say he's the *chairman* of the federation?"

Mr. McGuire beamed. "Yes, and it's quite an honor to have him do the test."

"This is unbelievable." I scooped up Hasenpfeffer and spun him around. "We're going to Scotland!"

"Make sure we're flying first-class," Hasenpfeffer said. "I don't do coach."

*"Hold on!"* Gram said. "You just can't go flying off to Europe on a whim."

"Not flying," Mr. McGuire said. "Through the mirror."

Gram stared goggled-eyed at him. "Go to Scotland *through the mirror?* Have you completely lost your mind?"

I bit my lip and looked at Mr. McGuire. He snapped the red suspenders drawn tight across his oversize belly. "It's cheaper than flying," he said meekly. "And quicker, too."

Gram threw her hands up in the air. "After what happened, I can't believe you'd even suggest such a thing!"

Hasenpfeffer sighed as I gently placed him back on the floor. "I guess this means another weekend cooped up in your room staring at unicorns frolicking on rainbows."

My shoulders slumped. Convincing Gram I should

travel overseas via a magic mirror that currently housed an evil magician would be next to impossible.

"I'm sure Mr. McGuire wouldn't send me unless it was safe to travel in the mirror," I said, not wanting to admit I was actually a little nervous about it myself.

Gram scoffed again. "You were seconds away from being *permanently* trapped in that mirror only two days ago under his watch, and now I'm supposed to give my blessings to use it to go to Scotland? This whole conversation is an utter waste of time." She pointed to Hasenpfeffer. "Get that infernal rabbit, and let's go home."

"Wait!" Mr. McGuire said. "After the Davenports' brought to light that Maggie might have been using her magic inappropriately at school, Viola Klemp thought it was imperative to get her licensed. Roderick Lachlan is an old friend of mine, and he agreed to add Maggie to his roster this weekend as a favor."

Gram waved her hand dismissively in the air. "Oh, Viola Klemp. Just because she had a little trouble getting sawed in half some forty years ago doesn't mean she can stick her nose into everyone's business. And since when does getting one's magical ability measured really matter? We all know Maggie's powerful." Gram glared at me with one eyebrow cocked. "She just needs to show some self-control."

It was a good thing Gram didn't know that I not only used magic to ace the entrance exam for my new private school but I'd also cast over a dozen spells to help my new friend Fiona Fitzgerald and me keep up with the class work. Of course, I wasn't even sure if Fiona and I were still friends—not after she'd figured out I used my magic to get her into the school too.

Mr. McGuire walked over to the counter and picked up a folder with my name written on it. "Actually, things have changed a bit in the last twenty years. The Society for Ethical Magicians has become quite powerful . . ." He paused. "There's been talk of having people stripped of their powers."

My stomach fluttered. "Could they actually do that? Take away my magic?"

Gram stiffened as the color drained from her face. "They wouldn't *dare!*" she snapped. "I won't allow it."

I stared at Gram in surprise, hardly believing my ears.

Mr. McGuire snapped his suspenders. "It was mentioned in the report that the Davenports were extremely concerned about Maggie's, um, reckless use of magic. If we get her tested and up-to-date with all the new magical regulations, Viola has agreed to just issue a warning."

Gram took the report and shuffled through the papers. "Does it have to be through the mirror?" she asked wearily as she placed the folder on the counter. "I think I could probably come up with the airfare if we cut back a bit."

My eyes widened. I couldn't believe she was actually thinking of letting me go.

"No need for that," he said. "I knew you'd be apprehensive about using the mirror for travel, so Sir Roderick and his wife have agreed to come speak with you about it." He looked down at his watch. "They're due to arrive in just a few minutes."

He rubbed his hands together. "Let's get the mirror ready."

"They're coming through the mirror?" I asked.

Mr. McGuire nodded. "What better way to demonstrate that mirrors are the safest mode of transportation?" He jogged over to the counter and picked up a canister labeled STABILIZER. He tilted it over a measuring cup, and I watched the cup fill with an iridescent blue liquid.

He looked up at me. "This stabilizer will keep the mirror from taking anyone in while it's being used as a portal. When I give the word, you pull the sheet off and I'll apply this."

I shuddered. If the sheet were simply pulled off the mirror, it would suck anyone and anything within a three-foot radius into itself—something I was not keen on experiencing again. And now that Hasenpfeffer's previous owner, Milo the Magnificent, was trapped somewhere inside, I figured it would be downright dangerous for me to enter without some sort of magical protection.

Gram fidgeted nervously with her hands. "Are you sure about this, Gregory?" She glanced at me, her face pale and pinched. "Are you sure that *man* won't be able to get out?"

"We've had the top magicians study the case. Milo isn't going anywhere."

He glanced at his watch again. "The stabilizer will allow the creation of a portal connecting to Sir Roderick's mirror in Orkney." He walked over and patted the mirror. "Maggie, on my count."

I gently grasped the top of the sheet. My heart revved up, and I hoped Mr. McGuire was right about Milo.

"Ready? Five. Four. Three. Two. One!"

I yanked the sheet off, and Mr. McGuire tossed the stabilizer onto the glass. The liquid sizzled and bubbled as it dripped down, evaporating into a blue steam that tickled my nose with a peppery smell.

Suddenly, I heard a seagull cry and the sound of waves crashing against rocks. A fishy, saltwater smell filled the room.

The surface of the mirror shimmered, and I saw a figure coming into view. I held my breath as Gram took my hand

and squeezed it tight. Finally, a tall man with wild, white muttonchops, dressed in a tartan kilt, stepped through the glass, and I exhaled, relieved to see it wasn't Milo.

The man bowed his head, turned back to the mirror, and reached a hand through it to lead out a much younger looking woman with dark, dewy eyes. She lifted the hem of her long, brown skirt as she awkwardly made her way over the wooden frame, and then shook out her hair, which hung past her shoulders like tangled, black seaweed.

The man ran a finger along his large, hooked nose and nodded. "Howz it gawn, Gregory? As ya can see, we made it in one piece. Will your Maggie be joining us this weekend?"

Mr. McGuire turned to Gram. "Margery, may I introduce Sir Roderick Lachlan and his wife, Rhona."

"Pleased to meet ya," Sir Roderick said. He held out his hand, and Gram took it hesitantly. "I wish I weren't wearing this thing," he said, pointing to his kilt. "But my dear Rhona thought it would make a good first impression. Hope you're impressed!"

"If it were me, I'd keep those knobby knees covered with pants," Hasenpfeffer said.

We all turned to my rabbit, who was peering up at Sir Roderick from the floor.

"At least you're wearing underwear," Hasenpfeffer added.

I cleared my throat, and he noticed us staring. His ears flopped. "Oops. Did I say that out loud?"

"I'm Maggie," I said. "And this is Hasenpfeffer."

Sir Roderick grinned. "Pleased to meet ya," he said to me. "And . . ." He looked down at Hasenpfeffer. "I think the wee bun will like the wild hares running around the castle grounds. That is, if Mrs. Malloy here gives the okay fer Maggie to come fer testing."

"Exotic locale *and* wild hares?" Hasenpfeffer whispered with a dreamy look. "Somebody pinch me."

Gram brought a hand to her chest, looking back and forth between the mirror and Sir Roderick. "I . . . I don't know about this."

"Maggie will be in good hands," Rhona said quietly with an accent I couldn't quite place. "But perhaps we can discuss this over tea. Would you care to join me at the castle, Margery?"

Rhona extended a pale hand toward the mirror.

"The castle?" Gram said, gaping at the mirror. "Me?"

Rhona tossed her long, black hair over her shoulders. "I would be honored to have you join me. It is only a short walk."

Gram wrinkled her brow. "What about Maggie?"

"I think it's best if you come with me and explore the castle yourself first. I know you're apprehensive about your granddaughter's safety, as I would be. Our daughter, Lyra, is just a few years older than Maggie, and Roderick and I would certainly want to make sure things were safe for her."

"Aye," Sir Roderick said. "Lyra is our world."

Gram turned to me and nodded. "Of course, but . . ."

Out of the corner of my eye I saw Sir Roderick flick a wand toward the mirror. The room was instantly filled with the smell of fresh baked pastries.

Gram sniffed. "Blueberry scones? My mother used to make those." She smiled wider than I'd ever seen; there was even a twinkle in her eyes.

Rhona shot her husband a look and sighed. "Hot out of the oven. Come. Everything will be *fine*," she said softly. "*Trust me.*"

Gram nodded. "Blueberry scones; we used to have them every Sunday. I'd almost forgotten."

Rhona took Gram's hand, and they stepped through the glass without even a wave good-bye.

"Well," Sir Roderick said after they'd vanished, "let's go over yer schedule for the weekend, eh? I have a list of reading materials for ya, Maggie. I trust you'll get to what needs to be done before next weekend."

"But Gram still hasn't said yes," I said.

Sir Roderick gave me a sly smile and winked. "She will."

# 4

## The Ties That Bind

"I can't believe you're getting out of the field trip to go to Scotland—through the mirror of all things!" Raphael said. He twirled his bagpipe practice chanter with his fingers and then pointed it at me. "You have all the luck—hopefully it'll be better now."

"I'll be with the chairman of the Federation of Magic, what could go wrong?"

"Knowing you? Everything."

I stuck my tongue out at Raphael. "Well, I was so excited about going to the Orkney Islands, I *totally* forgot about the school trip to Peaceful Planet. Ms. Wiggins will have a fit when she finds out I'm going to miss it."

Raphael laughed and brushed his brown curls out of his eyes. "I wish *I* were missing it. Do you know what it's like sleeping in a yurt with ten other kids who've all taken a vow of silence? Bodily function noises *really* stand out. I still don't know how Ms. Wiggins convinced the school we need to go on a mediation retreat every year."

A weekend at Peaceful Planet was just the thing our teacher, Ms. Wiggins, would be into. She alternated our insanely rigorous class work with insanely far-out mediations and new age teachings.

"So what's a 'yurt' anyway?" I asked.

"It's a circular, domed house originally used by nomads in central Asia. The whole weekend is a total snooze fest. Seriously, two hundred plus kids and not one sound uttered from Friday night until we leave Sunday afternoon. And they blast these depressing songs out of the loud-speakers twenty-four-seven."

"Like the whale chant CD Ms. Wiggins brought to class last week?"

Raphael nodded. "I wish I could go with you instead. It would be so cool to play my bagpipes in Scotland instead of my instructor's studio."

I leaned back in my computer chair. "I don't know for sure that Gram will say yes to the trip. She's still over there eating blueberry scones, but Sir Roderick seemed confident she would. I think he cast some sort of spell on Gram to convince her to visit the castle in first place."

Raphael gave an exaggerated gasp. "A magician casting a spell to influence someone? I'm shocked!"

I sighed. Raphael had been a lot more excited by magic until it almost got him killed. "Sometimes it can't be helped," I said.

"Yes, it can. And isn't that why you got in trouble in the first place—because Darcy found out you were helping Fiona in school with your spells?"

"How was I supposed to know Darcy was a magician—and that she'd figure out what was going on? Seriously, what are the chances there'd be *two* magicians in a class of eight kids?"

Hasenpfeffer jumped out of my lap and scowled up at Raphael and me. "For pity's sake, must you continue to say that horrible child's name? I'll probably have nightmares about her tonight."

He hopped over to his open cage and crawled under his blanket. I couldn't really blame him for being upset. Mrs. Davenport was Milo's cousin, and the last time Darcy had visited him she'd told Hasenpfeffer how much she'd like a pair of lucky rabbit's feet. Of course he had bitten her, but still.

"Anyway, *if* I can go to Scotland, I have to read these by Friday," I said, pointing to a small stack of books on my desk that Sir Roderick had given me.

"I think you should concentrate on what you're going to say to Fiona at school tomorrow," Raphael said. "Has she answered any of your e-mails?"

"No, but Max Litmann keeps sending me haiku about our participation in Milo's magic show." I turned in my desk chair and clicked on my inbox. "Here's *another* one." I sighed. "'Mirrors and magic, illusions to dazzle us, more than meets the eye.'"

Raphael stared at me. "'More than meets the eye'? Do you think he suspects you're a real magician?"

"Max? No, he's just hoping I'll tell him how they got it to look like I transported myself from one side of the stage to the other. And I don't think he's expecting me to say 'magic.'"

"Why isn't he asking *me* how I levitated above the stage?"

"He's already decided you had a hidden harness," I said. "I'll print the haiku he sent about it if you'd like."

Raphael rolled his eyes. "I wish I had been wearing a harness. But Fiona is who we should be worried about. She knows what you are, and we can't be sure what she'll do with that information."

I walked over to my bed and sat down next to Raphael.

"What information? That I'm a magician in training, or a magical cheater?"

"Actually, you're a little of both. But I've come up with a way to smooth things over with her."

"A spell so she'll forgive me?" I asked hopefully.

Raphael put his hands on his hips. "No. You wouldn't be in this mess if you hadn't been casting spells to make it look like Fiona was some sort of genius. Besides, this is better than magic." He hoisted the backpack he'd brought with him onto my bed. "I just happen to have the answer to the mystery of girl bonding in here."

I looked on expectantly as he unzipped the main compartment. He pulled out a handful of multicolored string and a bag of beads. "Friendship bracelets. The girls in class went nuts for these last spring."

"*Friendship bracelets?* I magically messed with her mind and you expect a bracelet to patch things up?"

"My cousin Paloma says they're like gold. Everyone wants one. When she came over yesterday, all she did was mass-produce them for her friends. She let me have some stuff to get you started." He held up the knot of tangled strings. "This will get Fiona to forgive you."

I shook my head. Fixing things with Fiona would take more than strings and beads. "I really think a little spell would do the trick."

"No magic!" Raphael said. "Make a couple of matching bracelets, throw in some hearts, and you two will be BFFs again in no time."

Raphael's cell phone rang, and he fumbled in his pack to get it out. "I'm coming, Mom," he said into the phone as he flung his backpack over his shoulder and flipped the phone shut. "I have to practice a new song my bagpipe instructor taught me today. If I don't, my mom won't let me work on my rodent experiments." He shook the bag of beads in my face. "Paloma *swears* this will work." He snatched his chanter off my bed and blew a few notes.

"You'd better go practice," I said, covering my ears. "You need it."

Raphael looked indignant. "It's not a flute; it's *supposed* to sound like that," he said, blowing one last sharp note before he left.

I gathered up the strings and beads and spread them out on my desk. I'd gotten a bracelet kit four years ago in second grade. I had trouble keeping the thin threads from tangling, and the beads kept slipping from my fingers before I could thread them. The one and only bracelet I completed unraveled five minutes after my friend Kate-Elizabeth put it on.

I pushed the beads around and then looked at the

books Sir Roderick had given me—*Guidelines for Magicians in the 21st Century, Avoiding Magical Mishaps, Ethics in Magic.* There was a small red book, *Elementary Spells for Children,* Mr. McGuire had slipped in too.

Mr. McGuire emphasized that I should read the first three books cover to cover, but if I had time, he thought I should practice some of the magic in Elementary *Spells for Children* before Friday. He thought it might look bad if I hadn't yet mastered what most magical kids had learned before they finished preschool.

I opened the red book and turned to the table of contents. As I scanned the list of spells, a smile came to my face. Weaving and knot-tying spells were on pages 44–47. I turned to the pages and quickly read through the spells.

This would be a piece of cake!

I sorted through the beads and picked out three special ones—a pink plastic seal for Fiona, since she loves animals; a red scarab to remind me of my parents, hunting insects in the Amazon; and a blue musical note for Raphael. I figured, since he was technically my best friend, he should get a bracelet too.

I untangled the threads and laid out enough for three bracelets. I was about to recite the weaving spell when I got an idea. I flipped through *Spells for Children* again, until I came to a friendship spell. I knew the book was seriously outdated—it had been Mr. McGuire's when he was a boy, after all—and casting a friendship spell was something that was probably breaking a hundred different "guidelines," but it wasn't like I was trying to be everyone's best friend. Raphael was already my friend, and until the magic show on Saturday, Fiona was too.

I flipped back and forth between the weaving and friendship spells and worked out a new one I hoped would combine the two. I needed one more thing—magic dust. I went to my closet and opened the door. I stood on my tiptoes and reached for a jar of magic dust number seven I'd borrowed from Mr. McGuire.

I carefully threaded each bead with nine multicolored strings and then sprinkled the yellow magic dust over them. I took my wand out of my desk drawer and pointed it at the beads. *"A spider weaves a braided trail, with charms of love that never fail, keep my friends forever near, keep my friends forever dear."*

My eyes widened as the threads rapidly wove in and out, forming multicolored, candy cane–like striped patterns around the beads. A minute later I picked up a purple and pink bracelet with a shiny pink seal bead in the middle.

"Best friends forever."

There was a knock on my door, and I quickly stuffed

the beads and bracelets in my desk drawer and put the bottle of magic dust behind my computer.

"May I come in?" Gram asked.

"Sure," Hasenpfeffer called out. "It's not like I was trying to nap or anything. Who cares if the rabbit is sleep deprived?"

Gram opened the door and walked over to me, ignoring Hasenpfeffer. "I saved one for you," she said, handing me a blueberry scone wrapped in a light blue linen napkin.

I took the scone and hoped it wasn't some sort of consolation prize for not being able to go to Sir Roderick's.

"So how was Scotland?" I asked nervously.

"It was lovely—lovelier than I'd imagined." She sat on my bed, folding her hands in her lap. "And I owe you an apology."

"You do?"

"As you know, magic is not all fun and games and rabbits being pulled out of hats." She looked toward the window and sighed. "There were some *things* that happened to your grandfather and me because of magic—things I desperately wished I could forget." She turned to me with tears in her eyes. "But unlike you, *my* wishes don't have any power. After your grandfather died, I cut magic out of my life and tried my best to forget the past—forget the magic."

"What happened, Gram?"

She shook her head. "It doesn't matter anymore. But I was wrong to try and cut magic out of my life and expect you to also. Magic can be *wonderful*, and it's affording you an amazing opportunity to spend the weekend in a castle on the coast of Scotland. You're a very lucky girl, and now that you know you have to use your magic responsibly, I know everything will work out."

Gram bit her lip as tears streamed down her cheeks. "I'd better get dinner going, and you have school tomorrow so I'll let you get to your work."

"But, Gram," I started.

She stiffened and sat up straight and tall. "Let the past *be*, Maggie. You just concentrate on having a safe and magical future working in the repair shop. And I don't want you to give the Davenports a second thought, because if they even *hint* about having you stripped of your powers again, they'll have to go through me."

I suddenly realized it was the Davenports' threat that had changed Gram's mind about magic. I would've thought she'd be happy to have a normal, nonmagical granddaughter; instead she was acting like a mother bear protecting her cub.

"Okay," I whispered.

Gram left and I looked all around my tiny room—and

at Hasenpfeffer snoring in his cage—and an overwhelming feeling of happiness started at the tips of my toes and spread up to my face until I was beaming.

I was going to Scotland, and I was allowed to work in the shop.

All I had to do was get through four days of school, convince Fiona I hadn't meant any harm when I messed with her head, and avoid the wrath of Darcy Davenport.

# 5

## Accelerated Learning

"I look so dorky," Raphael said as we walked down the hall to our classroom. "I may be a geek, but this is going too far." He held out his arm and shook his head at the blue and brown friendship bracelet wrapped around his wrist.

"This was your idea," I said.

"*For Fiona.* Not me. I'm manly—I don't do jewelry." He flexed his skinny arms, showing off the slightest hint of biceps.

"It's got brown in it, and I think it's a very manly bracelet for my very manly BFF."

Raphael blushed. "Fine, but if Max or Sal or any of the girls tease me, I'm taking it off."

"Deal," I said, holding out my bracelet next to his.

We walked into our classroom, where Ms. Wiggins, was dressed in an orange skirt with a matching vest covered with what I thought might be embroidered sheep. A huge fur hat sat on her head as she blew paint through a straw onto a white canvas. "Isn't this liberating, children?" she said after spewing a red streak onto the painting. "Working like this frees the mind from the constraints of conventional art and allows us to embrace our inner creativity and let off a little steam. Who would like to join me? It could be a collaborative piece."

Darcy Davenport ran her fingers through her frizzy blond hair as she stifled a laugh. "I think I'll just watch."

Her best friend, Serena Gupta, titled her head and examined the canvas. "It might be fun."

Darcy scoffed.

"Or not," Serena quickly added.

Ms. Wiggins took a deep breath and blew out a sprinkle of orange dots in a sweeping arc across the canvas.

"Hey," Serena said, looking back and forth between the painting and Darcy. "That looks like your freckles."

Darcy's face reddened as Max and Sal Perez came over to the painting.

"Yeah," Sal said. "It really does."

Max pushed his glasses up the bridge of his nose and stared at the painting. His fingers began to twitch in the air, a sign he was composing a haiku in his head. "From breath and color, Darcy's melanin we see, immortalized here."

Darcy's eyes bugged out as Nahla Jackson joined everyone by the picture, laughing.

Max grimaced as Darcy gave him the evil eye. "Um, not one of my best efforts, but really, it's an uncanny resemblance."

"Hey, everyone," Raphael called out. "What did you think of our show on Saturday?"

Ms. Wiggins turned our way, clutched her chest, and gasped like she was having a heart attack. "Our two brightest blossoming stars have arrived!" She rushed over to Raphael and me and swept us into her arms, hugging us tight.

Patchouli stung my nose as she pressed my face into her scratchy vest.

When she finally let us go, I saw her blink back tears. "Why didn't you tell us you were going to participate in the magic show?" She shook a finger in our faces before we could respond. "No. No. Don't say a word. I know you must have selflessly agreed to be in the show to help with the benefit."

Raphael and I exchanged looks and then nodded.

"Yeah, once we knew Milo the Magnificent was helping the local food pantries—which my grandmother volunteers for—we had to help," I lied.

Ms. Wiggins nodded as she waved her hands above her head. "Well, it was simply *spectacular*, and I'm still trying to guess how you pulled off those illusions. Not to mention your acting talent. I had no idea we had such thespians in our midst. Raphael, the look of sheer terror when you rose fifty feet above the stage was utterly convincing! And, Maggie—I truly believed you feared for your life while Milo pretended to have you in a choke hold." She sniffed and clapped her hands. "Bravo! Bravo!"

"Yeah, it's was a lot of fun," I said.

Ms. Wiggins clasped her hands under her chin. "I certainly hope they invite Milo back for an encore. I would willingly volunteer to assist him in his night of illusions."

She looked off into the distance. "I sometimes wonder if I could've had a stage career had I chosen a path that didn't involve nurturing children *one hundred and eighty days a year* for the last *twenty years*."

She suddenly froze and then let out a loud, blood-curdling wail that sent chills up my spine: "Aaaaaaaaaaaah!"

Max echoed with his own scream as he fell out of his chair in surprise.

"I'm so sorry, Max," Ms. Wiggins fussed as she rushed to help him up. "But as you know, when the muse calls, one must answer. Why, I almost believed I was in imminent peril myself."

She adjusted the fur hat on her head, threw her long hair over her shoulders, and jutted her chin out. "There's some untapped acting talent running through my veins, I just know it."

Max nodded as he rubbed the back of his pants before taking his seat again.

I peered behind Ms. Wiggins and saw Darcy scowling. Being the second cousin to Milo the Magnificent, Darcy knew firsthand that everything that had happened on the school's stage two nights ago was pure magic. She also knew Milo was trapped in Mr. McGuire's mirror and, therefore, unavailable for any further performances.

The rest of the kids crowded around us, and Raphael took charge, lying about things like invisible wires and mirrors to explain what had happened. I stepped back and saw Fiona staring out the window on the other side of the room.

I took a deep breath and walked over to her. "Hey," I said quietly.

"Hey," she said, still looking out the window at the Long Island Sound.

We stood in silence, watching boats sail past. A seagull swooped and crashed into the water before coming up with a small fish in its beak. I reached into my pocket and felt the bracelet I'd made for Fiona.

"I'm sorry I used magic to get you into the school," I whispered, "and to help you with all of the other stuff we did in class last week. I was just trying to help."

Fiona nodded. "I know." She kept staring out the window and sighed. "I wish you'd told me what you were doing, though. I thought I knew all this stuff and finally fit in here—and with my family." She shrugged. "When I figured out it was all magic, and I was still just *dumb* old me, I . . ."

I shook my head vigorously. "You're not dumb, and neither am I. We're just not *them*."

Fiona twisted one of her long, brown braids and looked at our classmates, who were still crowded around Raphael. "I *want* to be like them," she said in a hushed voice. "I want to be like my parents and my sisters, but I can't be that without you." She looked at me with sad brown eyes.

"Things have changed *drastically* since last Friday," I said, glancing at Darcy. "Let's go to the reading area and talk. We'll have to be careful—very careful—but I think I've figured out a way we can both fit in *and* stay out of trouble."

I told Fiona everything that had happened since I'd arrived in Bridgeport, Connecticut, over a week ago—discovering my grandfather had magical powers like me, finding Mr. McGuire's magic repair shop, Raphael and I heading off to rescue Mr. McGuire from Milo, and how the evil magician wound up trapped in the mirror at the end of the benefit show at our school. I told her about the wish magic I'd used to get us both into the Black Rock School, and that Darcy Davenport was also a magician—a magician who might be out to have me stripped of my powers.

When I'd finished, I gave Fiona the bracelet I'd made her. When she put it on, my own bracelet seemed to shiver and the scarab in the middle let off an eerie red glow for a second.

"I love it," Fiona said as she rubbed her fingers on the pink seal bead. "When I get to be a senator or congresswoman—whichever makes the laws—I am going to do everything I can to help protect seals from hunting."

"Speaking of seals, this weekend I'm going to an island off the coast of Scotland that is crawling with them. This guy, Sir Roderick, is going to do some magical testing to—"

"*Roderick Lachlan?*"

Fiona and I jumped. Darcy was standing on the other

side of the bookcases that made up the reading area.

My heart raced as Darcy stalked around the shelves and placed her hands on her hips. "Roderick Lachlan is booked for years. How did *you* get in? Your parents aren't even magicians."

"Sir Roderick is a friend of Mr. McGuire's," I said quietly. "And after *you* ratted me out, everyone thought I had to get tested ASAP!"

Darcy looked back and forth between Fiona and me with her fists clenched into little balls. "I 'ratted' you out because you were breaking all sorts of rules," she hissed. "You can't just use magic whenever you want to, you know."

"It's not my fault my parents aren't magicians and I didn't know about the rules. But don't worry, there won't be any more magic going on in school," I said, with my fingers crossed in my lap.

Darcy rolled her eyes. "You don't need rules to know you shouldn't use magic to get into a school that is *clearly* over your head." She looked down at Fiona. "Make that *heads*," she said, drawing out the *s* as if she were a snake.

"Yeah, well, from what Raphael's told me, I'll bet you've gotten more than a little help from magic dust number seven in the past."

Darcy laughed and played with the ruby locket

hanging around her neck. "Oh, please, magic dust is for losers who can't cast a decent spell with their own powers." She narrowed her eyes. "But I guess you would know." She flipped her frizzy mane over her shoulders and stalked off.

I groaned. "Like I said, we have to be careful."

"Don't listen to her," Fiona said. "She's just jealous."

"Yeah, but the sad thing is, I used magic dust number seven last night." I looked down at the bracelet circling my wrist and frowned.

"Well, that doesn't mean you *needed* it. And after that Lachlan guy does your testing, I know Darcy will be eating her words."

I nodded. But if I *had* tried a little harder, I probably wouldn't have needed magic to make the bracelets. My eyes traced the tightly woven threads, which made up an intricate pattern far better than anything I could've woven. Magic was hard to resist.

"Children!" Ms. Wiggins called out. "It's time for our morning meeting."

Fiona started to get up, but I put my hand on her arm. "Wait. I worked out a spell to help us. It will just give us enough of a brain boost so we'll know all the stuff they've learned at school. Once the spell takes effect, we'll be on a level playing field, but after that we're on our own."

"Really? You can do that," Fiona said, her eyes sparkling. "But . . ." She bit her lip and inhaled deeply. "I don't want you to get stripped of your powers or anything just for me."

I pointed to Darcy, who was bragging to Serena and Nahla about her "first place winning" science project she was working on even though the fair was still months away. "It's for *both* of us. And I think we can show these Black Rock kids that being smart isn't just about having a high IQ. If we know at least everything they do, there won't be any put-downs, and then we can figure out our own way to be 'blossoming stars.'" I waved my hands in the air and bugged out my eyes, trying to do my best Ms. Wiggins impression.

Fiona smirked. "Let's do it."

I gave the room a quick scan to make sure no one was around. I saw Raphael was sitting with Sal and my stomach turned guiltily. I knew he wouldn't approve of the spell, but he didn't know what it was like for Fiona and me being surrounded by pint-size super-geniuses. "How about a little magic dust number seven? For extra luck," I asked, taking a small vial out of my pocket. "Who cares what Darcy thinks?"

Fiona scoffed. "I don't. And it just so happens I'm a *huge* fan of magic dust number seven."

We leaned in close, and I pulled the cork off. I sprinkled some of the yellow powder onto our palms. Under the fluorescent lights, it shimmered like flecks of gold glittering in a running stream. "Ready?"

Fiona bit her lip and nodded.

I took her hand and squeezed it tight. *"Years of school we need to learn, knowledge is what we yearn, Serena, Sal, and all the rest, teach us both what they know best."*

I gasped as a jolt zapped my hand, and I pulled it back from Fiona's. Musical compositions, mathematical equations, foreign languages, and countless works of art flooded my brain. Famous faces flashed before my eyes as constellations twinkled in my head. Poems and chemicals mixed and churned into a final explosion that left me sitting wide-eyed and breathless on the rug.

"Fiona! Maggie!" Ms. Wiggins called out. "We're waiting for you. The talking stick is ready."

I took a deep breath and smiled at Fiona, whose flushed face smiled back in amazement.

"We're ready too," we said together.

# 6

## Ms. Wiggins Flips
## Her Lid

We gathered on the rug as Ms. Wiggins unwrapped the talking stick from the purple satin cloth she kept it in. No one was supposed to talk unless they were holding the stick, but from what I'd seen on the first two days of school, that rule was frequently ignored.

Ms. Wiggins cleared her throat. "Well, is there anything anyone would like to ask me?"

She looked at us eagerly. When no one spoke, she untied the earflaps of her furry hat and waved them up and down. "Any inquiries about my *outfit*, perhaps?"

Darcy let out a long sigh as she reached forward and

took the stick. "You're dressed as a Mongolian peasant because we'll be sleeping in yurts at the Peaceful Planet retreat, and you never miss an opportunity to find obscure topics to teach us. I'm also guessing you embroidered the sheep on your vest yourself."

Ms. Wiggins beamed. "One hundred percent correct! I studied the artisans of central Asia, spun my own wool, and embroidered a scene to represent the heart and soul of the traveling nomad." She stuck out her chest and waved a hand across her vest. "Behold the humble sheep."

We all stared at the misshapen creatures that appeared to be dancing across Ms. Wiggins's chest as she eagerly searched our faces for signs of approval.

"I feel an art project coming," Nahla groaned next to me.

Raphael shook his head. "In the sweat tank."

Ms. Wiggins took off her vest and passed it around the circle so we could get a closer look at her work. "I enjoyed the experience so much, I've asked your art teacher, Mr. Burns, to help us embark on an exploration of Asian textile weaving. Doesn't that sound like *fun?*"

A collective groan went up around Fiona and me.

Ms. Wiggins charged on, ignoring the horrified looks on everyone's faces. "To inspire you, we shall listen to a new CD by the Mongolian Songstresses. They're a musical group whose expressive voices re-create the gut-tural nomadic poetry and songs of central Asia. After we've immersed ourselves in music, we'll use your individual project time this afternoon to spin and dye wool, and then weave it into a pastoral scene of your own design."

Nahla raised her hand. "Did they move the art room over the summer?" she asked hopefully.

"Sadly, no," Ms. Wiggins said. "While I have continually pushed to have the art room moved to a more suitable location that would better foster your creative sides, it is, alas, still next to the boiler room in the basement."

She looked awkwardly at Fiona and me. "The school isn't as progressive about the creative arts as I would like—some foolishness to do with focusing on achievement scores and forcing elementary-age children to meet the standards of college graduates."

She took a deep breath. "But you can rest assured I will do everything in my power to see that you children get a rounded education that mixes the arts with the academics—even if it does get me another year of probation."

"I don't like weaving," Sal whined. "I was planning on reading my astrophysics book this afternoon."

Serena wrinkled her nose. "The art room smells like the wet cheese Max has on his sandwich every Friday."

Max sat up in surprise and pushed his glasses up toward the top of his nose. "Not *every* Friday!"

Raphael's shoulders slumped. "I was going to work on a new bagpipe song I'm composing—'The Rodents of Orkney.'"

We all turned and stared at him.

"You know I like mice," he said defiantly. "And I was researching the Orkney Islands of Scotland yesterday. It's fascinating. I could just picture standing on a craggy knoll overlooking the ocean, playing my bagpipes to my mouse, Pip."

Serena rolled her eyes, but Darcy didn't join her. I figured she knew I'd told Raphael about my trip to the islands, and she was still mad I was going for testing and not her.

"Ms. Wiggins, it's like an oven in the art room," Nahla griped as she eyed Darcy. "And I have a ton of work to do to get ready for the science fair next spring. I need to do research so I can successfully graft pear and apple tree branches onto one main trunk."

"I need to work on my project too," Darcy said, glaring at Nahla. "I know my mother would prefer I do that instead of *weaving*."

"Children!" Ms. Wiggins rapped the talking stick on the floor. "You will be creative, and you will *like* it." Her right eye twitched as she tied the earflaps of her hat back up. "And, Darcy, your mother might benefit from attending a Peaceful Planet retreat and discovering the calming influence of meditation."

"Speaking of the retreat," I said, thinking this was a good time to let Ms. Wiggins know about my alternate plans for the weekend, "it turns out I can't go."

Ms. Wiggins placed a hand over her mouth. "What? Not going? But this trip is crucial for your mental health. How else are you to center your being in preparation for the rigorous challenges you'll face this year?"

"I, uh, don't know, but I do have a note." I jumped up, ran to the coat closet, and took the letter Gram had written from my backpack. As I held the white envelope, I marveled again that Gram was letting me go to Scotland.

I handed the envelope to Ms. Wiggins, who proceeded to *tsk* over and over again as she read the note explaining that I had a relative visiting from out of the country.

I sat down next to Fiona, and she whispered, "I wish I was going with you."

"I wish you could go too. And it would be fun seeing Raphael playing his 'Rodents of Orkney' on an actual cliff in Scotland."

My bracelet seemed to tingle, and I gasped. I'd used the word "wish" again. Fiona smiled at me as my mind raced. She and Raphael were going to the Peaceful Planet retreat. There was no way they could go to Scotland even if I wanted them to. And sometimes wish magic doesn't even work. I felt the tension leave my body, sure this was one wish that couldn't possibly come true.

Ms. Wiggins placed the note in her lap and pouted. "What a shame. There's nothing like a seventy-two-hour vow of silence to really help you get in touch with your inner self. Well, at least the rest of us will be enjoying the blissful silence together."

Most everyone looked miserable, except Max, who was nodding his head at Ms. Wiggins. "I composed over thirty haikus last year. They're all in my second book, and my editor said it was some of my best work." He got a wistful look in his eyes, and his fingers began to twitch.

Darcy quickly poked him in the ribs. "If you come up with another haiku, I'll throw up." She caught Ms. Wiggins looking at her in surprise and smiled sweetly. "Because I'd hate to see him *wasting* all of his creative energy before the weekend."

There was a knock on the door, and Mrs. Davenport strolled into the room wearing a lime green suit. "It's awfully quiet in here. I hope I'm not interrupting anything of importance." She fluffed her short, blond bob and then looked quizzically at Ms. Wiggins's outfit. "It's not Halloween already, is it?"

Ms. Wiggins hopped up and swiped the fur hat off her head, leaving static-charged hair waving wildly around her face. She smoothed her long, dark hair with quick, jerky motions as she stared nervously at Mrs. Davenport. "We were just talking about this weekend's retreat. Just a few minutes ago I mentioned to your Darcy here that perhaps you might want to join us."

"Join you? Heh, heh," Mrs. Davenport tittered. "I mean, that's so very *sweet* of you to think of me, Alberta, but I have a million things to do this weekend."

"All the more reason to come. Sometimes the best way to cope with overscheduling is to leave it all behind and just meditate. We have an extra cot now that Maggie can't go."

Mrs. Davenport's narrowed eyes flashed to mine. "*Can't go?* What a shame, missing your first field trip at your new school."

I gulped. "I, uh, I have a relative coming in from overseas."

"From Scotland!" Raphael added.

Darcy folded her arms across her chest. "The Orkney Islands to be exact."

Mrs. Davenport's mouth dropped opened for a second, and then she resumed her wide, tight smile. "Orkney, you say."

"Yes, Mother," Darcy said. "The Orkney Islands, home of *Roderick Lachlan.*"

"Yes. I told Darcy I'm going to see my, uh, Uncle Roderick," I lied. "But I'll see him here in Bridgeport because there's no way I could go to Scotland for the weekend." I gulped again.

Mrs. Davenport's jaw clenched as her smiled thinned. "Isn't that *interesting*?" She tapped her fingers loudly against the pink clipboard clutched in her hands.

Ms. Wiggins beamed at all of us. "I'm so glad to see your classmates are getting to know you better, Maggie—all the more a pity that you'll be with your uncle instead of joining us."

I squirmed under Mrs. Davenport's glare. "Well, I'm sure the retreat won't be the same without you, Maggie," she said finally.

"Oh! I filled out the election form you gave me last week," Fiona said. "Let me get it for you."

I smiled gratefully as Fiona rushed off to the coatroom—glad the subject had been changed.

"I have mine too," Sal said. He looked at me. "Nahla and I take turns being secretary."

Nahla nodded as Sal left to get his form. "I'll run again next year."

"It's my year to run for vice president," Max said as he opened his notebook and handed Mrs. Davenport his paper. "Me and Serena swap."

"Lavonia Brown and I used to take turns being treasurer," Raphael added, "but now that she's moved, I guess the job's mine unless you want to take turns with me."

I shook my head. "No, I'm good. Why do you take turns instead of having a real election?" I asked.

"We tried running elections before, but it was always a boys-against-the-girls deadlock."

"Except for president. Wendell Skinner never wanted to do it, so Darcy always ran unopposed."

"But with me and Fiona here, there are more girls now," I pointed out. "And I think we're old enough not to just vote for our own gender."

Max didn't look convinced. "I'm happy switching."

"Me too," Sal said. "I have enough to work on without adding campaigning to my list of things to do."

Fiona came back and handed Mrs. Davenport her form. She gave it a once-over and then looked at Fiona with one eyebrow cocked. "Still have your sights on president I see. I guess it will be up to the class to decide if you or Darcy has what it takes to be a leader."

"Fiona wants to campaign to help baby animals," Serena said dreamily.

"Yes, dear," Mrs. Davenport said. "I recall you told me that on the first day of school."

Serena giggled. "I love baby animals."

"Oh!" Max opened a spiral notebook in his lap and flipped furiously through the pages. "I wrote a haiku for your campaign posters." He cleared his throat. "'Change is in the air, a kinder gentler regime, Fiona for prez.'" He blushed. "The last line needs a little work."

I cringed. It was obvious the spell I'd cast last week to encourage everyone to support Fiona in the election was still working. Darcy rolled her eyes as she tugged on her ruby locket, whose magical protection kept her from being influenced by the spell.

"I think that last line *could* use a bit more work, Max," Mrs. Davenport said. "But this is about *leadership abilities*, not baby animals or questionable forms of poetry. I'm sure Fiona will find something a little more pertinent to discuss when speeches are given next week."

Fiona paled as if she'd just realized what going head-to-head with Darcy in the election would really be like.

"I finished my speech over the weekend," Darcy said with a smirk. "I have a PowerPoint presentation, too."

"Do you want to save baby animals too?" Serena asked.

Darcy gaped at her. "You know what I want to do—you're my campaign manager, *remember*?"

A fog seemed to lift from Serena's eyes as she nodded her head. "Oh, yes, you're planning on—"

Darcy poked her. "Not in front of Fiona."

Serena bit her lip and nodded again.

Mrs. Davenport clutched her clipboard to her chest and fluffed her hair some more. "Anyone else?"

Everyone shook his or her head and Mrs. Davenport smiled again. "Well, then, I'll leave you to your work." She paused and stared at Ms. Wiggins. "I'm also looking forward to visiting the class again soon and seeing some actual *work* going on." Mrs. Davenport winked at Ms. Wiggins. "I know you're usually very busy. I must just keep coming at the wrong time. Toodles!" she said with a wave.

Ms. Wiggins stared at the closed door for a second and then took her furry hat off her desk and pulled it on her head. She made her way back to the rug and sat down wearily. "I've a bit of a headache. How about we listen to a little bit of the Mongolian Songstresses to unwind before we dive into our weekly 'mystery chemical' lab. I hope you all studied the periodic table of elements and their chemical interactions over the weekend. I have an extra copy of the Mongolian Songstresses' CD to award to the first person to correctly identify the chemical without blowing anything up."

Sal's face reddened as his hands flew up to his forehead and felt the ridges above his eyes.

"It's all right, Sal," Ms. Wiggins cooed. "Accidents

happen, and your eyebrows have grown back just fine." She zeroed in on Fiona and me. "We've studied the periodic table of elements in great depth. You two may just want to observe today."

Darcy giggled. "Or it could be fun to see what happens." She looked at Sal, raised her fists in the air, and then shot her fingers up straight. "Kaboom."

Sal hung his head, but thanks to my spell, I now had an in-depth knowledge of the periodic table of elements and I knew Fiona and I weren't going to blow anything up. I also knew I couldn't appear to know *too* much, so I chose my words carefully. "Actually, we did study chemicals in my old school—a little bit. Nothing like you guys, I'm sure."

I crossed my fingers and hoped Fiona would remember to play it safe.

"Me too," Fiona said. "I remember *something* about having to be very careful with *chlorates*. I *think* my teacher said they can be unstable, but I'm not a hundred percent positive."

I caught Darcy giving us the evil eye. "Maybe we should just observe today. I've never done anything with 'mystery chemicals' before, and I kind of like my eyebrows."

"Yes," Fiona said. "I think that's a very good idea.

"Chlorates *are* very unstable," Ms. Wiggins said, her

right eye twitching again. "But after what happened last June, I was strongly cautioned to use better judgment when giving out chemicals. So," she said with a laugh, "no one needs to worry about losing any hair or getting first-degree burns."

She untied the earflaps on her hat and rubbed the fur of the earpieces against her cheeks. "I'm still not sure a report documenting my so-called poor judgment needed to be added to my permanent file. Everyone was wearing safety glasses and protective aprons, after all. And it's not like they have teachers *dying* to work here." She shook her head at us for emphasis. "Between the low pay and the crazed parents demanding Harvard-level work from kindergarteners, one might say you'd have to be insane to even consider a teaching post here."

She continued shaking her head as she stared off into space.

"Would you like me to compose a haiku for you?" Max asked nervously after a minute or two of silence had passed.

Ms. Wiggins sat up, and her eyes grew wide as if she'd forgotten we were sitting on the rug with her. "Oh, no, no. That's very kind of you, but I'm all right. Let's just say I am counting the days until the retreat. Even teachers need to unwind and do some soul-searching."

She leaned over and pushed the play button on the CD player. A high-pitched string instrument cut through the air, joined by sharp, guttural voices. Ms. Wiggins closed her eyes and swayed back and forth. "Just relax. Picture yourself leading your flock of bleating sheep. Your yurt is packed tightly away on your horses' backs, ready for assembly, and you search the meadows for the ideal place for your next camp. Free your mind and explore the possibilities. And don't forget—though it pains me to do so, your weavings will be scored and their marks will reflect upon your world studies final grade for the semester."

Darcy tugged on Serena's sleeve. "Science fair," she whispered, and they both quietly got up.

Sal tilted his head toward Max. They crept away and stuck their noses in books they had left open on their desks.

Nahla sighed and played with one of her pixie braids for a few seconds, and then looked at the rest of us. "I've got research to do." She shrugged and tiptoed toward the computers.

Raphael pointed toward our desks. "She'll be out of it for a while," he whispered.

I looked at Fiona. "Do you want to check out the mystery chemicals? Maybe we can figure them out before the CD is over."

She shook her head. "Let's talk about Scotland."

# 7

## Unexpected Guests

Friday after school I stood in the repair shop, a suitcase at my feet, and looked at the cloth-draped mirror in front of me. As I reached out and felt the blue satin, a nervous tickle ran up my spine. I realized my legs were quivery and my underarms were soaked—and I knew why. Milo was in there, and he was mad. Mad at me because he thought I was responsible for sending him into the mirror. Everyone insisted it was safe to travel through it, but what secrets did the centuries-old mirror hold that Mr. McGuire or Sir Roderick didn't know about?

And had Milo discovered any of them?

I bit my lip to keep myself from wishing I were at the Peaceful Planet retreat with Raphael and Fiona. According to Raphael, they'd be sitting in their yurts listening to music and waiting for someone to deliver a "light dinner" consisting of something inedible, like dried figs and gluten-free bread. The kids left the yurts only to use the bathrooms, which were really outhouses without running water.

I reached out with a shaking hand to touch the fabric again. I felt the wooden frame under the satin and tried to sense some sign of danger.

Nothing.

I shook my head to chase away the bad feeling. I really didn't want to go back into the mirror. "Do you think it's safe?" I asked Hasenpfeffer.

He stopped gnawing on the edge of the wooden counter and sat up on his haunches. "What? That mirror? You're grandmother was in there, right? If the old bird says it's okay, I'm good."

"It's not like Gram knows a whole lot about magic, though."

Hasenpfeffer snorted. "For pity's sake, just be grateful she's letting us go and we can get out of this dive for a while. I used to be a world traveler, you know. I'm not used to being in one place this long."

*"I know."*

"Where's McGuire?" Hasenpfeffer asked as he hopped around the mirror. "I'm dying to taste the grass in Scotland. The grass overseas is always so much better than here in the States."

*Here in the States.*

At that moment I wanted nothing more than to stay in the States with Gram.

With my fingers I traced the embroidered moon and stars on the fabric covering the mirror. There was still a lot I had to learn about magic, but I'd seen enough to know things could go wrong—terribly wrong. And when I'd met Mr. McGuire, he'd told me I needed to trust my intuition. I dropped my fingers to my side.

My intuition was telling me not to go.

But if Sir Roderick Lachlan, the head of the Federation of Magic, said this was safe—and Gram agreed—who was I to question them? Besides, with the Davenports gunning for my powers, what choice did I have?

The repair shop door opened and Gram walked in with Mr. McGuire. He placed an old, worn suitcase on the floor next to mine and then snapped his red suspenders. "Are you excited?" he said to me.

"I guess."

Gram wrung her hands and walked toward me. "You

do whatever it takes to do well on your test." She tugged at the tight bun on the back of her head, and then whisked away some stray gray hairs from her face. "Don't forget to use your best manners. You're staying at a castle after all, and Mrs. Lachlan is very formal."

"I will."

She looked at me wistfully. "I'm sorry I won't be able to accompany you—and sorry to miss out on some more of those heavenly blueberry scones."

"That's okay. I know you have to run the food drive."

She nodded. "We do need to start pushing for donations now if we want to be sure we're well stocked for our Thanksgiving baskets."

"I'll take good care of her," Mr. McGuire said. "Oh, I talked to Sir Roderick before I left my apartment. He said there's quite the storm brewing over there. And it'll be dark when we arrive, so I have flashlights for us to use in the mirror."

"Flashlights?" I said. "I thought we'd be coming out of the mirror in his castle."

"We will," Mr. McGuire said. "But the portal uses the natural light of the time zone we'll be going to. I'd say about midway we'll need to turn these on."

Mr. McGuire checked his watch. "Okay, we should be on our way."

I picked up a flashlight from the counter. "Do you want me to carry you?" I asked Hasenpfeffer.

He kicked his back legs out and then shook his head. "I'd rather hoof it on my own if you don't mind. I haven't had a good run in ages."

I looked awkwardly at Gram, not sure if I should hug her good-bye.

She leaned in and patted me on the shoulder. "Good luck. I can't wait to hear what level you come out at. I bet it'll be a whopper."

"Thanks," I said.

Mr. McGuire rubbed his hands together. "It's time. You pull the sheet on my go, and then I'll throw the stabilizer on. Ready?"

I nodded.

"Go!"

I yanked the sheet off, and Mr. McGuire tossed the blue stabilizer on the glass. It sizzled and steamed like before, and I could see the surface of the glass ripple like water.

I gulped and picked up my suitcase. "Do you want me to go first?" I asked Hasenpfeffer.

He scoffed. "Scotland here I come! Try not to miss me too much, Granny," he said as he leapt into the mirror. "See you on the other side," he called out as he disappeared.

Gram wrinkled her nose. "For the hundredth time,

I'm not your grandmother!" She put her hands on her hips and frowned. "It wouldn't break my heart if you encouraged him to take an extended stay in Scotland."

I laughed. "He just may want to do that—Bridgeport seems to be cramping his style."

"I'll go next," Mr. McGuire said. "Once you step through, we'll just have a short five-minute walk to the castle. Good luck with your food drive, Margery. We'll see you on Sunday."

I watched him walk into the mirror and bit my lip.

"I know you're nervous," Gram said. "But I wouldn't let you go if I hadn't made the trip myself."

"I know," I said softly.

Gram tilted her head toward the mirror. "Better be off. No doubt Hasenpfeffer is already making a nuisance of himself."

I walked up to the mirror and took a deep breath. As I stepped through the surface, the hair on the back of my neck stood up and a faint electrical buzzing flitted over my skin. The last time I'd been in the mirror it had been filled with a cold, blustery fog—one that hid eel-like creatures with sharp teeth. Now I found myself at the start of a long, mirror-lined path that curved up ahead and no sign of Mr. McGuire. I could hear ocean waves crashing in the distance, and I jumped when a crack of lightning followed by a deep, rumbling thunder shook the walls.

"Mr. McGuire? Hasenpfeffer?"

I started down the path and my shoulders slumped when I turned the corner and saw another empty corridor. The light was fading fast so I turned on my flashlight.

"Hey, guys, wait for me!"

"Here," a voice whispered behind me, followed by another crack of lightning. "Finally here."

My heart pounded as I spun around. "Mr. McGuire?" I shone the flashlight along the walls, but all I could see was my frightened face reflected endlessly in the mirrors.

I caught a glimpse of a shadow out of the corner of my eye and turned back around.

"So close," the voice said. "So very close."

I swallowed hard and started quickly down the path with my suitcase bumping against my leg. A cool wind whipped toward me carrying a fishy-smelling fog that flooded the narrow passage. Thunder rumbled up ahead, and I realized my flashlight was starting to dim. I shook it and the light flickered for a second but stayed on.

"So tantalizingly close," the voice hissed from seemingly all around me.

I gasped. It was Milo's voice—I was sure of it. I ran full speed, turned another corner, and saw that the path split in two up ahead.

*I knew going in the mirror was a bad idea*, I thought as I tried to catch my breath. More thunder rumbled, and my flashlight sputtered and went out. *"I wish the flashlight was working!"* I said hurriedly.

Nothing.

I shook the flashlight in frustration. "Mr. McGuire!"

"You're all alone," Milo whispered. "Well, not quite. I'm here and so very happy to see you."

I froze in the dark, trying to figure out what to do. Suddenly the scarab on my friendship bracelet began to glow.

"Hello?" a familiar voice called out. "Is anyone there? Anyone who can tell me where I am?"

"Raphael!" I shrieked as I felt along the wall. "It's me, Maggie. You're in the mirror. Keep talking so I can find you."

He groaned loudly. "I should've known you had something to do with this. I'll hold out my wrist—my bracelet is glowing; look for the blue light."

"Maggie? Raphael? Is that you?" a quivering voice called out.

"Fiona?" I gasped. "You're here too?"

"I'm scared," she cried out somewhere ahead. "What's going on? How did I get here?"

Lightning illuminated the corridors for a second,

and I saw I had reached the fork in the path. As the darkness returned I could see the glow from their friendship bracelets bobbing up and down in each of the misty passageways.

I held my own bracelet up. "Walk toward the red light."

When they reached me, we all held up our bracelets. Our faces were bathed in the colored lights, which had grown stronger now that we were together.

"What did you do this time?" Raphael asked. "I was lying peacefully on my cot listening to Sal Perez snoring—seriously, he conked out the minute his head hit the pillow—and then bam! I'm in the pitch dark with lightning zapping around."

Fiona nodded as she twisted one of her braids. "Me too, and I don't feel so good."

"I'm so sorry, guys, but I *think* I may have accidentally wished you here."

"Think?" Raphael demanded.

"That, combined with the spell I cast on the bracelets, could've done it. The exact wording included the phrase 'keep my friends forever near.'" I tried to smile. "Oopsy."

Raphael glared at me and threw his hands in the air. "'Just make the bracelets,' I said. 'Everyone *loves* bracelets. You don't need magic,' I said. And what do you do? Cast a spell that gets me ripped out of my yurt and trapped in the mirror."

"Look, whatever spell I cast isn't important. What's important is we figure out how to get out of the mirror— *Milo is in here.* Didn't you hear him?"

Fiona's eyes popped. "Milo? The guy from the magic show—the one who tried to kill you both?"

"Yes, he's in here somewhere. He was talking just before you showed up. You must've heard him."

Raphael shook his head. "I didn't hear anything." He looked at Fiona.

"Me neither."

"Did you actually *see* him?" Raphael asked nervously.

"Well, no."

We all stood in silence for a few seconds looking up and down the corridors, waiting for our eyes to adjust to the dark.

"Maybe you just thought you heard him," Fiona said quietly. "You were pretty worried about coming in here." She looked around some more. "You know, power of suggestion."

Suddenly the passageway flooded with light. Mr. McGuire, followed by Sir Roderick charged toward us.

"Maggie!" Mr. McGuire cried, as he and Sir Roderick held out their wands blazing with light. "Where have you been and what happened to the portal? Did you cast some sort of spell?"

"No! It was Milo. When I entered the mirror, there was just this long, crazy path of mirrors and no you. He's in here, though, I heard him." I crossed my fingers, hoping he'd believe me.

Mr. McGuire exchanged looks with Sir Roderick.

"Apparently Milo's been a busy fella, eh? He's certainly been making the most of his time trapped in here. Well, let's not dawdle. Let's get ya out of here. You and your friends, that is."

Mr. McGuire peered behind me and his mouth dropped open. "Raphael? And who is this?"

I sighed. "This is Fiona. Remember I told you about her? I kind of accidentally cast some spells, and they kind of accidentally showed up."

Mr. McGuire groaned. "Oh, Maggie. Your timing couldn't be worse."

Sir Roderick laughed. "Ah, lighten up, Gregory. You Americans take everything so seriously. There's nothing wrong with a young magician playing around with magic. And don't fret just 'cause the Davenports are joining us this weekend."

"Darcy?" I said in unison with Raphael and Fiona.

"Ah, yup, the little bugger's mum badgered me for

an invite. She was quite persistent actually. But come on, let's get out of here before Milo figures out how to break through this portal he altered."

"Am I really going to Scotland?" Fiona asked.

Sir Roderick smiled. "I never say no to unexpected guests, and it's probably not the best idea to be lingering in here till we get things figured out."

He pointed his wand like a sword down the right corridor. *"Change of scene, places to roam, show us the path that leads me home."*

The walls teetered and seemed about to collapse on us. Fiona let out a squeal and I lifted an arm over my head protectively, but as the mirrors fell they turned into a fine powder that blew around with the dissipating fog.

A lush oriental carpet appeared under our feet, and the walls were now lined with large, gray stones instead of mirrors. Torches hung burning up ahead, and I breathed out a sigh of relief.

Sir Roderick waved a hand toward the shimmering opening of the mirror. "Welcome to Dark Craig Castle."

# Say Cheese!

I stepped through the mirror and gaped at the room we were entering. Giant tapestries hung on the walls depicting scenes of men hunting unicorns and ships sailing in seas teeming with monsters. Large floor-to-ceiling windows lit up as lightning flashed, and I caught a glimpse of a storm-churned ocean pounding on the rocks outside.

I searched the room for Hasenpfeffer and finally spotted him snoring peacefully on a large bearskin rug by a dying fire—apparently unconcerned for my welfare.

Mrs. Lachlan rose from a plush chair and walked to

her husband's side, looking inquisitively at Raphael and Fiona. "What is this, Roderick? There are more children to test?"

Sir Roderick laughed as he stroked his wild gray beard, which jutted out like a billy goat's. "No, just some strays young Maggie picked up on her way here. There's been a wee bit of trouble with the mirror, so we can't be sending them home till it gets sorted out. Good thing we have the room to put them up."

Mr. McGuire snapped his suspenders. "They can't stay; their parents will be frantic looking for them."

"Actually," Raphael said. "Our parents think we're at the Peaceful Planet retreat. We were supposed to take a vow of silence and spend the weekend meditating in our yurts."

Sir Roderick shook his head. "You Americans have the *craziest* ideas of fun, but this should be an easy fix. We'll just erase you from the memory of everyone at the retreat, and no one will be any the wise—"

"We can't do that!" Mr. McGuire interrupted. "Mind enhancements are highly unethical."

"McGuire, when did you get to be such an old fuddy-duddy?"

I turned around and saw a man with dark, slicked-back hair and bright blue eyes standing just inside the room. He was wearing a leopard-print bathrobe over a pair of yellow silk pajamas and had a pipe in his hand. A sleek black cat wove in and around his slippered feet, purring loudly.

"This can't be the same Gregory McGuire," the man said with a stiff English accent. "Not the one who spiked the punch at the 1966 Magician's Convention, turning everyone blue, and later went on to cast a spell on the guest speaker so his talk was interrupted by repeated flatulent outbursts?"

Mr. McGuire turned beet red as he stared at the man in surprise. "*Ian Shaw*, what on earth are you doing *here?*" He looked back and forth between Ian and Sir Roderick's wife.

Mrs. Lachlan hung her head and left her husband's side to gaze out the darkened window.

"I've brought my nephew Munro," Mr. Shaw said. "He just turned fifteen and all his friends have their federation licenses and he wanted one as well. I have to say I was excited to hear it was you barging in on his private testing, Gregory—we've been out of touch for far too many years."

Mr. Shaw adjusted the tie on his robe, and then took a puff on his pipe. He blew out a series of large bubbles that popped as they drifted up toward to the ceiling.

"Had to give up the tobacco—not good for the lungs," he said when he caught me gawking at him.

"We'll have another child coming through a photograph soon. That's how the Davenports will be arriving," Sir Roderick said.

"You can travel through a photo?" Fiona asked, looking at us with wide eyes. "Really?"

Mr. Shaw shook his head and leaned in toward Mr. McGuire. "This one's not going to score real high, eh?" he whispered a little too loudly.

"She's *not* a magician," Mr. McGuire said, and then he pointed at Raphael. "And neither is he. They're friends of Maggie's. She's the one taking her test. She's Gerry Malloy's granddaughter."

"Well, children," Mr. Shaw said, "you're in for a treat! Not many ordinary citizens are privy to the goings-on in a magician's castle. You've both been sworn to secrecy, right? I'd hate to have to turn either of you into a toad, as it's a rather difficult spell to pull off. Can't tell you the number of times its come off badly."

Raphael gulped. "I won't tell a soul!"

"Me neither," Fiona said, rapidly shaking her head.

Mr. Shaw laughed. "I was teasing. Most nonmagical people keep quiet about this sort of stuff to avoid being forced to endure psychiatric care of one sort or another.

I hear electroshock therapy is quite nasty. As for you, Gregory, I must say I'm surprised you allowed yourself to be dragged out of that quaint little repair shop of yours."

"Well," Mr. McGuire began, "Maggie here ran into a bit of trouble, and Viola Klemp thought Roderick should do her testing—"

Mr. Shaw snorted with laughter and bubbles popped out of his nose. "Viola Klemp? What's she on about this time? She thinks she can boss everyone around just because she started her little Society for Ethical Magicians. If you ask me, she's bitter because she's only a level nine and jealous of those of us doing tricks with a full deck of cards, so to speak."

Sir Roderick tilted his head back and laughed. "Or she's afraid someone will saw her in half again."

He and Mr. Shaw dissolved into a fit of guffaws and black slaps.

I couldn't believe what I was hearing. I'd thought Viola Klemp was someone with a lot of authority, but it was obvious Mr. Shaw and Sir Roderick considered her a bit of a joke.

Mr. McGuire snapped his suspenders. "Really, gentlemen, there's a lot to be said for using magic responsibly. Look what happened to Milo," he said, pointing to the mirror. "And we're here because his cousin Mrs. Davenport alerted Viola to some possible magical transgressions Maggie may or may not have been a part of. They *insisted* she be tested."

Mr. Shaw raised an eyebrow and ran a hand over his slick-backed hair. "Not Delilah Davenport?"

"Yes," Mr. McGuire said. "Do you know her?"

"Too well," Mr. Shaw said with a nod. "She's always signing up for committees and trying to take them over. But I know for a fact," he said, giving Mr. McGuire a conspiratorial look, "that her husband, Eugene, is a notorious scoundrel when it comes to using magic to improve his finances."

Sir Roderick pulled on his beard. "Most unfortunate-looking fella too—frizzy hair, bat-like ears that stick up a mile high. Wouldn't be at all surprised if he used a love spell to snare Delilah."

Mr. Shaw turned and looked wistfully at Mrs. Lachlan. "That was probably the smartest thing Eugene has ever done."

Mr. McGuire clucked his tongue and wiped his brow with his red bandanna. "We're *supposed* to be setting a good example for the children. And Viola Klemp is expecting Maggie to come away with a better appreciation for the proper use of magic from the chairman of the federation."

"You're absolutely right, Gregory," Sir Roderick said. "It's time I let Maggie in on the secret all upstanding magicians know." He marched toward me like a soldier. "As chairman of the Federation of Magic, it is me duty to tell you this . . ." He leaned in so close I could see the gray hairs poking out of his nose. "If you're thinking of casting a spell you shouldn't, make *darn sure ya don't get caught.*"

Mr. Shaw slapped his knee and laughed some more, while McGuire rubbed his temples with his fingers. "Roderick, Ian, *please.*"

"You know what we did at the last Federation of Magic meeting, Gregory?" Sir Roderick asked.

Mr. McGuire shook his head wearily.

"We played cards and drank a delightfully aged bottle of scotch. No one in the federation takes Viola and her little society seriously—not overseas at least."

"But she said there have been cases where people petitioned to have other magicians stripped of magic. The Davenports implied they might do just that to Maggie."

"'Petitioned' is the key word," Sir Roderick said. He scratched his hairy chin and winked at me. "We read the things, and then toss them out. You didn't actually think we'd strip someone of their power, did you, Gregory? We're not monsters after all."

"But I don't understand," I said, feeling both relieved no one was going to try to take my powers away and a little confused as to why I'd had to make the trip to Scotland. "Why do I need to get a license, then?"

"So you can show it off to all of your magician friends and brag about who's more powerful, of course," Sir Roderick said. "Gregory, you know what it's like being a magician. The Society for Ethical Magicians and the federation can make up all sorts of rules and bylaws, but at the end of the day, how are we to stop anyone from casting a spell? It's not like we can tell the authorities—not unless we want to get carted off to the nut house."

I looked at Mr. McGuire. I'd come all this way through a mirror—a mirror Milo had apparently hijacked—for nothing.

He sighed. "I'm sorry, Maggie. I had no idea. Viola made it seem like it was imperative. She does take her job very seriously, and I guess I wrongly assumed everyone else did as well."

Sir Roderick folded his hands across his chest. "Viola Klemp is an old woman who dreams of a perfect world of magic that's just not possible. I'm sorry I brought ya here under false pretenses, Gregory. To be honest, I thought ya were just looking for an excuse to get out of that repair shop of yours for a change of scenery."

"I was!" Hasenpfeffer called out.

We all turned to see Hasenpfeffer sprawled on his back with his hind legs in the air.

"Jinx!" Mr. Shaw said sharply. "That rabbit is *not* dinner!"

Hasenpfeffer rolled over and let out a squeal as the black cat sprang up from its hiding place behind a chair and leapt toward the rug.

Mr. Shaw whipped out a wand and pointed it toward the cat. "Don't make me use this," he called out.

The cat changed course and landed neatly next to Hasenpfeffer on the bearskin rug, and then looked back innocently at Mr. Shaw. It then proceeded to knead the rug for a few seconds before curling up into a ball as if it had only wanted to warm itself by the fire and had no interest in the rabbit that also just happened to be there.

Hasenpfeffer scowled at Jinx and then hopped to the far end of the rug. "Cats," he muttered. "No one told me there'd be cats. I'd have thought twice about making the trip if—"

"Roderick," Mr. McGuire interrupted, "why bring the Davenports all the way here by *photo* of all things?" Mr. McGuire asked.

"'Cause I knew I'd never have another moment of

peace if I didn't. Delilah Davenport is like a bulldog. She latched onto the idea I should test her Darcy as if it were a bone. I knew she wouldn't give up till I agreed."

"Hey, look," Raphael called out. "On that table—those flashing lights."

"That must be the Davenports arriving; shouldn't you put the picture on the floor?" Mr. McGuire asked.

"Nah." Sir Roderick chuckled. "After all the badgering I've gotten this week, I want to have some fun."

Fiona nudged me. "What's happening?"

"Darcy is traveling to Scotland by photo," I whispered. "I read about it in one of the books Sir Roderick gave me."

Fiona beamed. "I can't believe this; it's amazing."

"No, it's crazy," Raphael said.

I stared at the bright lights shooting up from the photo like a flashbulb on a camera going off repeatedly. "He's right. Crazy is more like it. From what I've read, I'll take traveling in a magic mirror housing an evil magician over going by photo *any day*. But maybe traveling two-dimensionally isn't as bad as it sounds."

Raphael stared at the flaring light bursting up from the photo. "Two-dimensionally? This I have to see!"

Suddenly, Mrs. Davenport's head—no wider than the width of a piece of paper—jutted out of the picture. She twisted and turned, until her shoulders were out as well.

Her head swelled like a balloon until it returned to its normal shape, and then she reached her paper-thin hands out and pushed against the tabletop. "Isn't someone going to help me?"

Mr. McGuire rushed to the table, and she reached out a flattened hand. He took it and started to pull. Mrs. Davenport managed to wriggle out onto the long wooden table, where her body plumped out and returned to its normal size.

"I suppose you think this is funny having me crawling up here?" she spat, as she slid off the table and tried to smooth her usually well-coiffed hair.

"Oh, no," Sir Roderick said calmly. "It's just we didn't think you'd be arriving so soon."

Mrs. Davenport looked at her watch. "It's nine o'clock your time—*exactly* when I said I'd arrive."

Darcy's squished head poked out of the photo. "Mother!" she wailed.

Mrs. Davenport rushed to her side. "Hold on, baby!" She moved the photo to the floor and reached down to tug Darcy up by the scruff of her shirt.

Darcy grunted as her mother pulled, and her skinny neck stretched three times longer than normal. Darcy finally reached a hand out and clawed at the rug as her mother continued to pull.

Once Darcy was out and back to normal, the two of them glared around the room with red, sweaty faces.

"Welcome, ladies," Sir Roderick said. "Glad you could make it."

Darcy's eyes became wide as saucers when she noticed Raphael and Fiona.

"Hey!" Raphael said with a wave.

"Bummer traveling by photo—from what I hear, mirror is the way to go," Fiona added.

Mrs. Davenport glared at the mirror. "We could've gone by mirror?" she sputtered breathlessly. "I thought it was broken."

Mr. McGuire looked sheepish. "It was, but I repaired it. Had I known you were coming I certainly would've offered my services; although, there was a bit of a mishap."

"Mishap?" Mrs. Davenport said as she straightened her jacket and smoothed her pants.

"Maggie ran into yer cousin Milo," Sir Roderick said. "Well, heard him anyway. He's figured out how to alter the inside of the mirror."

Mrs. Davenport put a hand to her mouth. "Perhaps he's close to finding a spell to get himself out of that thing. Wouldn't that be wonderful, Darcy?"

"Whatever," Darcy muttered as she fanned her face.

I noticed the journey through the picture had added a

great deal of volume to her already frizzy hair, exposing the bat-like ears she must have inherited from her father. Her mother caught me looking and rushed over to Darcy wielding a hairbrush she'd just taken from her oversize purse.

"I told you to put your hair up in a ponytail before we left," she said, yanking the brush through Darcy's matted curls.

"Mother!" she shrieked, ducking away. "I can do my own hair!"

Mrs. Davenport stood up straight and smiled angelically at her daughter. "Of course you can, *sweetie*, it's just that you never do and we're in the chairman of the Federation of Magic's *castle* in front of all these people, for goodness sakes."

Mrs. Lachlan turned away from her post by the window and walked slowly toward Mrs. Davenport. I noticed her eyes looked red and swollen like she'd been crying. I looked at the dark window, trying to figure out what she might have seen that would upset her. When a crack of lightning lit up the night, I thought I saw a figure walking on the beach.

Mrs. Lachlan held out a hand to Mrs. Davenport. "Welcome, Delilah. I'm Rhona Lachlan, and I'm so very happy to have you and your daughter joining us for the weekend."

"Thank you, Rhona. We're delighted your husband so graciously found room to fit us into his busy schedule." She turned to Mr. Shaw and eyed him up and down. "And thank you, Ian, for allowing us to crash your nephew's testing. I must say I was quite surprised to hear *you* were going to be here."

Mr. Shaw puffed on his pipe, sending bubbles drifting to the ceiling. "Can't imagine what you mean, Delilah, but be sure to tell Eugene I said hello."

"Mrs. Davenport," Mr. McGuire said nervously as he gave her a little wave. "Before we go any further, we have a little problem you might be able to help us with. It seems Fiona and Raphael *accidentally* accompanied Maggie here. Do you think you might be able to take them back to Bridgeport through the photo, and then drop them off at the Peaceful Planet retreat?"

Mrs. Davenport gave him an incredulous look. "Do you know how *expensive* the ingredients are to make up the potion for photographic travel?"

"As a matter of fact I do," he replied. "I stock the ingredients in my shop—not that you stopped in to purchase any."

"They're cheaper online," she said, looking down her nose at him. "And from what I'd seen of your little *shop*, I wasn't sure if you had the freshest stuff on hand."

Mr. McGuire raised his eyebrows and put his hands on his hips. "My shop may be old, but I can assure you everything I stock is in tip-top condition!"

"Um, excuse me," Fiona said, raising her hand like she was in school. "After seeing them arrive, I don't think I *want* to travel by photo. If it's all the same to you, I'd like to stay until the mirror is fixed and do what Sir Roderick said—you know, alter people's memories."

"It's the best thing, really," Sir Roderick said softly. "Just a harmless memory adjustment."

"I can't condone that!" Mr. McGuire said as he gave Mrs. Davenport a sideways look. "It's wrong—*very wrong*. And we always follow the rules. Always have. Always will, because we're a bunch of rule followers." He took his bandanna out and wiped it across his brow again.

Mr. Shaw stifled a laugh, and I wondered if he was again thinking about Mr. McGuire turning a roomful of magicians blue.

"You know what?" Mrs. Davenport said, rubbing her temples. "I have a splitting headache I can't magic away. And frankly, these other children are none of my concern. The only thing I want to think about is finding my room and getting some rest."

Mrs. Lachlan nodded. "I'll show you to your room at once. Perhaps the children should go to the game room while you gentlemen discuss the best course of action."

She led Mrs. Davenport out, and Sir Roderick stroked his beard. "Don't you fret," he said, looking at Fiona and Raphael. "We'll make sure no one at that retreat is missing ya. Head down the hall to the third room on the left, where you'll find Munro puttering around, I'm sure. And perhaps my Lyra. The two have been spending quite a lot of time together."

I gave Fiona and Raphael a hopeful smile. "I guess you're spending the weekend in Scotland—isn't that great news?"

Fiona looked around the room and nodded. "I keep pinching myself to see if I'm awake and not dreaming it all!" She laughed.

Raphael sighed. "Before this weekend is out you might wish this were a dream." He folded his arms across his chest. "With Maggie's luck it's only a matter of time before something happens, probably something bad. The only question is when?"

# 9

## Zap!

"Figures you botched up a spell and brought these two along," Darcy said as we entered the game room. "You're a walking magical disaster."

"Who is?"

We all stopped short. A tall boy was leaning against a pool table in the center of the room. My stomach fluttered. He looked like a movie star—with dark, wavy hair, bright blue eyes, and dimples on either side of his dazzling, white smile.

Darcy pointed in my direction, not taking her eyes off him. "Maggie is."

He tapped the pool cue on a white ball, knocking an orange one into a corner pocket. "Nice to meet you, Maggie," he said, with an English accent. "I'm Munro Wallace Shaw. I suppose you're the lot taking the test with me."

"Uh-huh," I managed to squeak out.

I suddenly realized Fiona was gently tapping me on the arm. "Introduce me," she whispered.

I nodded. "This is . . ." My mind scrambled to come up with her name.

Raphael cleared his throat, and I turned to see him rolling his eyes. "*Fiona!* Her name is *Fiona.*" He shook his head. "I'm Raphael Santos. Fiona and I aren't here for testing—we just came along for the ride."

"*I'm* Darcy Davenport," Darcy said as she tried to smooth her frizzy hair down. She strutted to the other side of the pool table, rolled a ball toward Munro, and then batted her eyelashes. "Maggie completely messed up some spell and got them dragged here by mistake." She giggled "Can you *believe* it?"

My cheeks flushed and I almost wished I were back in the mirror, but Munro turned to me and smiled wider.

"I have a reputation for casting disastrous spells myself. In year six I almost burnt my school down when I tried to magically pinch the answers for a test and the papers caught on fire. Then in year nine I tried to cast a love spell on Jordanna Pennysworth; it misfired and hit my teacher instead. Talk about embarrassing. Lucky for me, my uncle Ian is a bit of a scoundrel himself, so he wasn't mad."

He winked and my stomach flip-flopped.

Darcy put her hands on her hips, obviously disappointed Munro didn't think I was as magically hopeless as she did. "Well," she said, "I'm looking forward to the testing tomorrow. My mother suspects I'll score as high as a level twenty-five. That's better than anyone in my family and just about everyone I know." She gave me a sideways glance.

When she redirected her attention to Munro, Raphael and I exchanged looks.

"Twenty-five?" he whispered to me.

I shrugged as a he stifled a laugh. We knew I was at least a level fifty because I had the ability to magically transport myself. Darcy obviously hadn't figured that out or she never would've agreed to come to Scotland and get shown up by me.

Suddenly the double doors leading to the outside burst open and a rain-drenched girl with long, tangled dark hair stumbled in from the storm with the wind howling after her.

"Lyra!" Munro cried, running to her side.

Raphael and I rushed over and fought the gale to shut the doors behind them as lightning flashed nearby.

"I was wondering where you were. What on earth where you doing outside on a night like this?" Munro asked her.

She clung to him and shook her head. "Sometimes I can feel the tide pull at me to go to the ocean's edge. I get like that sometimes—I don't know what comes over me. I just can't stop myself."

"You're shaking," Munro said. He brought one of her hands to his face and pressed it tightly against his cheek. "And frozen solid. Let me get the fire going to warm you up." He led her to the hearth and used his wand to start a roaring fire. Then he cast a spell and dried her soaking clothes.

"I'm Maggie," I said, sitting on a couch nearby. "And this is Fiona and Raphael." Raphael smiled awkwardly at her. "Hi."

Fiona sat next to me and gave Lyra a little wave. "Hi. We're not here for testing, though."

Raphael nodded

"Hello," Lyra said breathlessly. She turned to Darcy. "And you are?"

Darcy took a seat in a plush chair, eyeing Munro as

he sat next to Lyra. "I'm Darcy Davenport. I *am* here for the testing—my mother and I arrived a short while ago by photo."

"Oh," Lyra said. "I've only once seen someone arrive by photo, years ago. It looked like a positively frightening way to travel."

Darcy smiled and sat up taller. "It's not so bad as long as you remain calm."

"She's a tough one, eh?" Munro said, looking at all of us for confirmation.

I rolled my eyes—Darcy had seemed anything but calm coming out of that photo.

Munro reached out and took one of Lyra's hands. "Of course Lyra here, braving the storm, is no slouch either."

Lyra smiled at him. "I love the storms. I love the way they toss the waves with extra ferocity." She looked longing at the glass doors facing the ocean. "The sound of the surf pounding the shore is like music to my ears."

Munro laughed. "It's the thunder and lightning I'd be worried about."

"I don't mind it," Lyra said, leaning into Munro. "It just makes it all the more exhilarating." She giggled.

Darcy's face clouded over as she watched them coo and laugh. "Wow, not afraid of thunder and lightning. Bet you're an ace at Zap."

"Zap?" I asked. "What's that—some kind of spell?"

"It's a game," Darcy said.

Munro looked puzzled. "I thought everyone played Zap across the pond. It's an American import after all."

"Just ignore her, Munro," Darcy said. "Maggie's from one of those families where magic skips a generation—the list of things she's clueless about is infinite."

Munro looked at Darcy with skepticism. *"Infinite?"*

"You know," Fiona said, "immeasurable, countless, inestimable."

"I know what it means." Munro laughed as Fiona's cheeks turned candy apple red. "I was just thinking," Munro continued, "that Maggie here is more on the ball than she's being credited for. You have to admit that was one spectacularly powerful spell she pulled off—being able to hoist two chums from their houses and bring them to Scotland and all."

"Actually," Raphael said, "we were at a meditative retreat with our classmates, but 'hoist' is an accurate description of the feeling I got when I was forcibly yanked from my bed and—"

"I'm not sure you can categorize a spell as 'spectacular,'" Darcy interrupted. "Not when it was completely unintentional. I'd say it was more of a *colossal* screw-up."

"No," Munro said. "I stand by my original assessment.

I can't imagine pulling off that trick—even loaded down with magic dust number seven. I for one would bet the Queen's crown that Maggie here shows us *all* up on the test tomorrow."

Darcy glared at me as if I'd cast a spell to put words in Munro's mouth that would embarrass her.

"Well, if you have such a high opinion of Maggie's talent, why don't we see how '*spectacularly*' good she is at Zap, then?"

"You think that's wise?" Munro asked. "It takes a lot of practice to get the hang of Zap."

Darcy wrinkled her nose at me. "I'd bet the 'Queen's crown' she'll do just fine—you know, since she's so '*spectacular*.'"

Munro smiled his dazzling smile at her. "Hey now, I didn't mean to imply *you're* not a talented young magician too, Darcy."

"Young?" Darcy scoffed. "I'm twelve years old—I'll be thirteen in two months!"

Munro laughed and Darcy huffed and popped her eyes in anger. "I'm sorry," he said, holding his hands out in front of him. "I didn't mean to offend you, but Lyra and I are fifteen and the lot of you look like young pups to me."

Darcy stood tall with her hands on her hips. "I happen to be a *very* mature twelve, but why don't we let Maggie decide if she wants to play or not?" Darcy pointed her nose in my direction and sniffed. "You *do* want to play, don't you?"

I looked back and forth between Darcy and Munro, unsure what to say. "Um—I guess," I finally said.

"Great," Darcy said. She turned to Lyra. "You'll play too, right?"

Lyra shook her head. "Oh no, I've never played." She looked down at her lap. "Let's just say I'm not like my father," she said quietly.

"So I've heard," Darcy said.

Lyra's brow furrowed. "Heard?"

Darcy's face flushed. "I, uh, just meant it's obvious you take after your mother."

"You *are* the spitting image," agreed Munro.

I stared at Lyra for a second and wondered if she'd been skipped by the magic gene like my father had.

"Well, let's get started and see who will take the Zap crown." Darcy whipped her wand out from her back pocket and pointed it at my feet.

"Hey, what are you doing?" I asked, taking a step back.

She shook her head, ignoring me, and started a spell. *"Three's the number for this game, Zap attack till one remains."*

Suddenly, three brightly colored square mats and three silver wands appeared at my feet.

Munro walked over and picked up the wands, giving one to Darcy and one to me.

"All right, then, take a platform and we'll spread out," he said. "Ten paces."

"Don't you think you should explain the rules to Maggie before you start?" Raphael said.

I nodded as the cool metal wand in my palm chilled my hand.

"It's simple," Darcy said. "You stand on the platform, point your wand at one of your opponents, and say 'zap.' An electric jolt of magic will hit the person and hopefully knock them off-kilter a bit. If you drop your wand or step off the platform, you're out."

I stared in horror imagining Darcy sending a lightning bolt's worth of electricity at me, making my hair stand on end and smoke come out my ears.

"She forgot to tell you that you *get* as good as you *give*," Munro stated.

Raphael raised his eyebrows. "So you don't want to go too hard on your opponent because you stand as much chance of flinching as they do—cool!"

"Not cool," Darcy said. "White. Hot. Zap!"

I gulped. "Maybe I'll just watch you two."

Darcy's upper lip curled up in a condescending smirk. "I wish I could say I'm surprised you're too *chicken* to play, but I'm not."

"Cut her some slack," Munro said. "I'd be a bit nervous too if I hadn't played before."

"Yeah, maybe you *should* just watch, Maggie," Fiona said. "This doesn't sound like a very nice game."

"No one ever said Zap was nice," Darcy stated.

I looked at Darcy, who was still smirking at me. "I'll play. How hard can it be?" I said, trying to sound braver than I felt.

Darcy smiled gleefully and shot a hand in the air. "I call first!"

"Great," I muttered. I picked the blue platform and counted out ten paces. I turned and saw Darcy on the pink platform and Munro on the green.

Darcy pointed her silver wand at me. "We go counterclockwise until only two people are left. That means you're my target."

My shoulders slumped. I wasn't surprised she was going after me, but I had really wanted to see how the game worked before it was my turn to get "zapped."

Darcy planted her feet a foot apart on her platform and licked her lips. She narrowed her eyes, took a deep breath, and shouted, *"Zap!"*

A white light shot out of the tip of the wand and I braced myself for the impact. A jolt struck me across the cheek, leaving a searing pain that throbbed like a bee sting. *"Ow!"* I shrieked, wobbling unsteadily for a second. "I thought we'd be starting out slowly!"

"And you're supposed to aim below the neck," Munro said.

Darcy feigned innocence. "Oops, I forgot. We usually skip that rule when I play with my cousins. I'll remember next time, but if you thought *that* was bad, you're not going to last long. You better make your first shot a good one, because you might not get another turn."

I rubbed my cheek and then pointed my wand at Munro.

"How much emphasis you put on the word 'zap' will determine how bad I get hit," he said. "And don't let Darcy psych you out. Big talkers like her usually burn out fast in Zap."

"Or they go on to win," she said coolly.

I looked at Raphael and Fiona and they nodded their heads in encouragement. I knew I should start out slowly, but I also didn't want Munro to think I was a wimp— not when Darcy was already shooting hard. I squeezed my hand around the base of the silver wand and pointed it at Munro. He moved his shoulders up and down a couple of times and bent his knees slightly to get ready for the hit.

I moved my wand around, trying to figure out where to aim, and finally zeroed in on Munro's chest. "Here goes," I said.

"Don't warn him, you dimwit!" Darcy declared. "Just do it."

"*Zap!*" I cried. An electric shock of white-hot pain raced up from the wand in my hand, across my shoulders, and down my other arm, sending blue sparks sizzling out of my fingertips. A high-pitched yelp escaped my mouth as my hands trembled. I felt the wand slip from my grasp, and I stumbled backward as I fumbled to catch it.

"Maggie!" Fiona and Raphael cried. They ran to my side to catch me, but we all tumbled to the floor in a heap at the same time my game wand did. We let out a collective groan as the wand—and my platform—disappeared in a puff of blue smoke.

"You're out!" Darcy hooted.

"But it was a *bloody* good shot!" Munro said breathlessly as he rubbed his chest. "Unfortunately for you, it was a little *too* good. Can't say you didn't give it your all."

"*Classic* newbie mistake," Darcy said. Without even waiting for us to get up, she shook her head at me and then turned to Munro. "Looks like it's just you and me."

Munro cocked his head. "Can't say I like playing Zap

with girls—usually it's with me and my chums and things can get pretty rough."

Darcy pushed up her sleeves and readied herself on her platform. "Girls are just as tough as boys!" She glanced at Lyra. "At least some of them are. Bring it on."

Munro flashed his smile. "All right, then." He took aim at Darcy and said, "Zap!"

A light zinged out of his wand and then bounced off the top of Darcy's shoes. She rolled her eyes. "That was a mistake you'll regret," she told him.

"What happened?" Fiona whispered as we stood up.

"I think he went easy on her," I said, "and if I'm guessing right, she's going to hit him with all she's got."

Darcy eyed Munro and shifted her weight back and forth on her feet. She jutted out her bottom lip, pointed her wand, and then screamed, "Zap!"

An explosion of light blasted out of her wand and hit his left knee. His body tensed as he stifled a yell. "You're tough all right," he said through clenched teeth.

Sweat dripped down Darcy's forehead, and I knew that jolt was probably a hundred times worse than what she'd sent at me.

"I was right," Fiona whispered. "This isn't a nice game."

"But it's right up Darcy's alley," Raphael added.

I rubbed my throbbing cheek. "You won't get an argument from me."

Darcy smiled at Munro. "Don't hold back this time."

Munro pursed his lips and dragged his sleeve across his forehead. "What do you say we call it a draw, eh? I don't want either of us to get hurt."

"Yes," Lyra added. "Why don't you stop? I can't say I'm enjoying watching this."

"What's the matter, Munro?" Darcy asked. "Scared I'll win? Scared you'll get beaten by a *twelve*-year-old?"

Munro stared at Darcy. "I'm not scared; I just don't want to hurt you. My mates and I don't even play the game this hard."

"Well, I do, and I say take your best shot!"

Munro sighed and pointed his wand at Darcy. "Have it your way, then. Zap."

A bolt of light clipped Darcy's shoulder, and she immediately fired back. *"Zap!"* she cried.

An explosion of white magic shot at Munro, hitting him squarely in the chest. His eyes widened and he stumbled backward off a platform and landed on his backside.

"I win!" Darcy pumped her fist in the air as Munro's platform disappeared in a sizzle of green smoke. She pushed aside the hair sticking to her sweaty cheeks and smiled triumphantly.

Lyra rose from the couch, but Munro held out his hand. "I'm okay." He nodded at Darcy as he pushed himself off the floor. "Wait till my chums hear about you—you'll be legendary. I think my reputation will take a bit of a knocking, though. Getting bested by a twelve-year-old will definitely get me some ribbings. "

Darcy beamed. "I'm really not *that* much younger than you, Munro." She batted her eyes again, and Fiona and I exchanged a look. "And," she continued, "I have to say, you were a most worthy opponent. I wasn't even sure I was going to be able to beat you. I mean, it was obvious you were holding back, but you took my hits a lot longer than most people. I think you and I are a lot alike—we're both tough."

"I don't know about that," Munro said. "I do know I'll take Zap over the thunder and lightning any day." He plopped down on the couch, and Lyra started to fuss over him.

"Where does it hurt?" she asked.

He smiled faintly at her. "'Where doesn't it?' is the question."

Darcy stared down at Lyra and Munro with narrowed eyes. I could envision the wheels turning in Darcy's head. Munro might respect her tenacity, but it was obvious the girl leaning into him by the fire was the one who had his heart and no amount of showing off during a silly game was going to change that.

An uneasy feeling spread through me because I knew Darcy would find a way to make Lyra pay for commanding all of Munro's attention.

She approached Lyra and Munro with a nasty one-sided smile, and I could tell she was choosing her words carefully. She finally sat down on a couch opposite me and gave Lyra a questioning look. "It's not really so surprising you feel at home on the beach—even in a storm like this. I mean, just because you're a *halfbreed* doesn't mean you can ignore the call of the sea."

# 10

## The Shape-Shifter's Curse

"Darcy!" I cried. "What a thing to say."

"Yes," Munro said as he put an arm protectively around Lyra. "What's this nonsense?"

"Oh my," Darcy said, bringing her hand to her mouth in fake surprise. "I just assumed you knew—especially you, Munro. With Ian Shaw being your uncle, I figured he would've told you all about him and Mrs. Lachlan."

Munro's brow furrowed. "Mrs. Lachlan and my uncle?"

Lyra sat up and pulled back her long, dark hair from

her face, her eyes flashing with anger. "What are you getting on about?"

"Well . . ." Darcy twirled a finger in her hair. It was obvious she was enjoying being the center of attention. "It seems your uncle was in *love* with Mrs. Lachlan—before she *was* Mrs. Lachlan. When he met her twenty-five years ago, he tried to steal her away from Sir Roderick. According to my gammy Davenport, he loved her so much he didn't even care about Mrs. Lachlan's condition or *the curse.*"

"Curse?" we all said at the same time.

Darcy nodded. "Yes, curse. When Gammy found out my mother and I were coming to Dark Craig Castle, she tried to talk us out of it because she knew how dangerous it could be."

Lyra pushed herself up and stood over Darcy. "Perhaps you fancy yourself a storyteller, but I won't stay here and listen to your schoolgirl nonsense a second longer!"

Darcy jumped up and blocked her way. "It's not nonsense! Gammy even showed me an old book that talked about the curse—and a lot more, too." She turned and glared at all of us. "But maybe I should just let you all fend for yourselves," she said finally. "Even though your lives could very well be in danger."

"Come on, Darcy, a curse?" Raphael said skeptically.

Darcy nodded. "The shape-shifter's curse."

"What's a shape-shifter?" Fiona asked.

"Not a what—a *who*," Darcy said. She took a step closer to Lyra. "A shape-shifter is a supernatural creature that can assume another guise, like a werewolf . . . or even a person."

"Shape-shifters aren't supposed to be real," Raphael said.

Darcy raised her eyebrows. "Neither are magicians."

"But . . . ," Fiona began. Her eyes were wide and frightened and I thought she might be thinking this trip to Scotland wasn't so great after all. "But what's the curse? You said we could be in danger."

"Do you really want to know?" Darcy asked.

We all looked at one another, and it was clear everyone wanted to hear the story, even if no one would admit it.

When no one protested, Darcy sat back on the couch, and Munro guided Lyra to a plump chair. Munro sat on the floor at Lyra's feet, and we all looked expectantly at Darcy.

"A hundred years ago," she began, "the previous owner of the castle, Duncan Catherwood, fell in love with a selkie named Oona and asked her to be his wife."

"What's a selkie?" Fiona asked.

"A selkie is a seal creature who can remove his or her pelt and assume human form," Munro said. "They're supposed to populate the coasts of the British Isles."

Darcy nodded. "Oona's father was against the marriage, but Duncan swore their love was so strong, she could have her sealskin back whenever she wanted and he trusted that she would always return to him.

"Unfortunately, after they were married, the honeymoon *quickly* ended. Duncan saw how restless his new bride was. He'd watched her sitting at the ocean's edge staring out into the sea—seals bobbing in the distance. And he worried she might not come back if she were ever again to don her pelt and feel the cool ocean currents against her sealskin. Thirty days after Oona pledged to be his wife, she asked for her sealskin, and Duncan Catherwood refused to give it to her or divulge its hiding place."

Fiona put a hand to her mouth. "But that's awful. He made her a prisoner."

Lyra nodded in agreement and turned her head toward the doors she had entered through. The wind-driven rain splattered noisily against the glass as tears gathered in her eyes. Her lower lip trembled, and I couldn't help thinking how much she looked like her mother staring out at the black ocean earlier that evening.

"Oona soon fell ill," Darcy continued. "She begged her husband for her sealskin so she could visit her family one last time. He refused her again, and she went mad. Sick with fever, she ran to the beach and threw herself into the churning waves, trying to find her way back to the selkies. She was frail and the seals tried to keep her afloat, but her heavy skirts soaked with water were too much for them and she was pulled under." Darcy looked us each in the eye. "And she drowned."

Lyra let out a sob.

Darcy looked at Lyra and a half smile came to her face. "That night Oona's father came to the castle in human form. Selkies have mysterious magic as old and powerful as the oceans, and when Duncan opened the door, Oona's father cursed him and anyone else who would keep a selkie from their pelt, saying they would meet a tragic death.

"The next morning, Duncan Catherwood was found dead with a key clutched in his fist. They say it looked like he'd been attacked by an animal in his bed—his pillow and sheets were shredded and deep claw marks were found gouged into the windowsill. Some of the servants swore they saw a large, dark cat the size of a panther racing away from the castle. They did track down a large chest in the attic that the key opened, and there they found Oona's sealskin—too late to be of help, though. The shape-shifter's curse had already come true."

Munro laughed. "Interesting tale, but what's it got to do with us?"

Darcy smiled. "According to my Gammy, Mrs. Lachlan is a shape-shifter. More specifically, a *selkie*, and any time now the curse could come true."

We all glanced at Lyra as Munro's smile quickly faded. "What a lot of nonsense," he said.

Darcy shook her head rapidly, making her frizzy hair bounce. "No. She's a selkie and my gammy said if you look closely at her hands and feet you'll see they're webbed. And did you see her looking out the window earlier? I'd bet anything she was wishing she was in the ocean with the other selkies."

Lightning flashed across the sky, and I wondered if it was actually possible that Mrs. Lachlan really was a selkie and missed her family like Oona had. Was Sir Roderick keeping her skin secreted away so she wouldn't leave him?

"How *dare* you spread such vicious lies in my own home?" Lyra said, getting to her feet.

"Don't pay any attention to this rubbish, Lyra," Munro said, standing by her side. "She's obviously nutters."

"I'm telling the truth!" Darcy declared. "My grandmother said that when your mother isn't wandering the castle searching for her skin, she walks the ocean's shore crying over the selkie family she'll never be with again."

Lyra pointed a finger at Darcy, her face contorted with anger. "Stop it this instant."

Darcy's face flushed, but she stared up at Lyra with grim determination. "Sorry to be the bearer of bad news, but your mother is a selkie—and that makes you one too," she said calmly.

Lyra shook her head as tears welled up in her deep brown eyes. "This is utterly preposterous!"

Darcy cocked an eyebrow. "It also means you have a seal pelt hidden somewhere in the castle."

"You're wrong," Lyra cried, but as tears streamed down her face, I wondered if she suspected it might be true.

"I could be," Darcy said, "but I don't think I am. Gammy Davenport went to school with your grandmother Gemma Lachlan. They kept in touch, and Gemma called her years ago with the news that your father was going to marry a selkie."

Darcy looked at all of us. "As you might imagine, selkies don't make the best spouses—what with suffering from wanderlust and all—and she was concerned that Sir Roderick was making a huge mistake. Sir Roderick insisted he'd never keep your mother away from her pelt like Duncan Catherwood had, but on the day you were born he snapped and hid her pelt—yours too."

"Darcy, *stop*," I said. "Please!"

"Yes, we've heard enough of this foolishness," Munro said.

Darcy stood up and glared us. "I'm not lying!" She turned to Lyra. "You said it yourself, 'Sometimes I can feel the tide pull at me to go to the ocean's edge.' And what about your mother? Does she endlessly search the castle, going in and out of rooms, up to the attic and down to the basement, opening closets and chests of drawers? Does she skulk along the beaches? Does she watch the seals?" Darcy held out a hand. "Are her fingers *webbed*?"

Lyra bit her lip and looked down at her own hands. She slowly spread her fingers, revealing a hint of webbing between the base of each finger, and her face crumpled. She shook her head and balled her hands into fists. "It can't be true. They would've told me."

Darcy shrugged. "Parents don't tell their kids a lot of things."

We all sat in silence. I looked at Lyra and saw the hurt and confusion on her face. "Don't listen to Darcy," I said.

"Yes," Raphael said as he brought his knees to his chest. "And statistically speaking, if the curse was real, something would've already come to pass."

Darcy looked indignant. "I'm only repeating what my

grandmother told me—and she believes the story is true and that we all could be in danger."

A log on the fire popped, sending up a cascade of sparks.

Lyra spread her fingers again. I could see her hands shaking as she held them up to her face, the webbing in clear view. She looked toward the sea and a single tear rolled down her cheek. "I have to go."

"I'll come with you," Munro said, putting an arm around her.

Lyra ducked out from under his arm and raced out of the room. "No. I need to do this myself."

"Lyra!" Munro called out, looking heartbroken.

"So," Darcy chirped. "Anyone want to play pool?"

Munro glowered at her. "You must be seriously *joking!* And I don't know what's worse. The fact that you felt the need to tell Lyra this ridiculous story, or that I sat here and let you do it." He stalked out of the room.

Darcy's cheeks flushed, but she forced a smile on her face. "Well, at least I just saved him a whole lot of heartache in the future. And who knows, maybe a younger woman is what he needs."

"We have to do something," Fiona said, ignoring Darcy.

"Something as in avoid getting attacked?" Raphael said.

"No, we have to find Mrs. Lachlan's and Lyra's seal-skins."

"Fiona," I started, "even if the story is true, don't you think Mrs. Lachlan would've already turned the castle upside down looking for her pelt? And if Sir Roderick really did hide her pelt, he most likely would've used *magic*, making it impossible to find."

"And I can't see how it's any of your business anyway," Darcy added.

Fiona put her hands on her hips. "You made it my business!" she snapped. "And a week ago I would've sworn casting spells and going to Scotland through a magic mirror was impossible. Now that I know anything can happen, what kind of a person would I be if I didn't try to help?" She looked at all of us. "*Anything* is possible, Maggie. You and Darcy are magicians, and Raphael is a certified genius. How hard would it be to figure out where the sealskins are hidden?"

Hasenpfeffer raced into the room. "For pity's sake, could someone please tell me what's going on?"

"What do you mean?" I asked, though I had a feeling news of the shape-shifter's curse was already traveling through the castle.

He hopped over to me, giving Darcy a wide berth. "I was trying to nap because I was feeling a bit jet-lagged."

"Jet-lagged?" Darcy rolled her eyes. "How can you get jet-lagged traveling through a mirror?"

Hasenpfeffer sniffed and twitched his nose at her. "Rabbits are very sensitive to travel—whatever the method. *Anyway*," he said turning back to me, "I was lying peacefully by the fire on that delightfully warm fur rug when all heck breaks lose. Some girl is yelling about secrets, Mrs. Lachlan is crying about her *selkies*— whatever they are—and Sir Roderick is shouting at Mr. Shaw for dredging up the past. Mr. Shaw is demanding Sir Roderick reveal the location of some sort of skins, and to top it off, that infernal black cat kept eyeing me hungrily and licking its lips. I just had to get out of there. This is not at all what I signed up for when I agreed to come to Scotland. I was expecting a relaxing vacation and scenic vistas, and now my tummy is upset. Did you bring parsley?"

Fiona looked at us with wide eyes. "It's true, then. They really are selkies."

I threw my hands in the air. "I hope you're happy," I said to Darcy. "You just had to butt your way into my trip and ruin everything for everyone!"

"You don't own Scotland—I have just as much right to be here as you. At least I didn't bring a bunch of tag-alongs," she said, waving at Fiona and Raphael.

"Hey, I didn't ask to come," Raphael said. "I told Maggie not to use any more spells."

I turned to Raphael. "I know! Sorry for messing up your life *again*." Tears sprang up in my eyes. "This whole trip is a joke. I don't even *need* a license, but Darcy had to go complain to Viola Klemp because I cast a few spells—like magicians aren't doing just that *all the time!*"

"About that parsley?" Hasenpfeffer said.

Fiona stamped her foot. "Everyone be quiet!" Her chest rose and fell in rapid succession. "I didn't ask to be here either, but here we are—all of us. And maybe Darcy should've kept her mouth shut, but don't you think Lyra's better off knowing what she really is? Maybe now she can convince her father to give the sealskins back. And maybe then Mrs. Lachlan can make her own choice about where she wants to live, instead of being *trapped* here in the castle."

She put her hands on her hips and jutted out her chin. "The bottom line is, these people need our help, and we have to give it to them."

"You can go all Girl Scout on this if you want," Darcy said. "But *I'm* going to bed." She smirked. "Sleep tight, and don't let any wild animals *bite*."

# 11

## Teeth and Claws

After Darcy left, Hasenpfeffer chattered his teeth noisily. "This is *so* not the vacation I'd planned. I should be feeling rejuvenated, but with all the tension in this castle I hardly have the energy to keep my ears up. Droopy ears are *not* a good look for a rabbit."

"We have more important things to worry about than the state of your ears," I told him.

"You don't need to rub it in. I know I'm just a rabbit— a nobody, *a speck of dust*. On a scale of one to ten I wouldn't be at all surprised to learn I'd rate a zero with you."

"That's not true," I said. "It's just . . ." I looked at

Fiona. "We have to help the Lachlans—this is bigger than all of us."

Fiona nodded. "Right, and like you said, Mrs. Lachlan has obviously searched the castle thoroughly."

"So there's no sense in us wasting time duplicating her efforts," Raphael said. "Being a supernatural creature doesn't mean she has the ability to cast a spell to locate her sealskin. That's your department, Maggie."

"So you know any good spells?" Fiona asked.

"Yes!" I said. "I read how to cast retrieval spells in a book Mr. McGuire gave me to study for my test. I practiced transporting apples from the kitchen. The spells are a little wordier than normal, but it was easy."

Hasenpfeffer snorted. "I wanted her to retrieve the parsley from the produce bin in the fridge, but did she listen to me?"

"You ate two apples without any complaints," I said.

"But I *prefer* parsley."

I ignored his last comment and took out my wand. "Give me a minute to work out a spell." I bit my lip and turned the words around in my head so they'd be just right. "Okay," I said, smiling at Raphael and Fiona. "I think this just might work."

Fiona beamed, and she and Raphael held their hands up in the air, fingers crossed.

I lifted my wand aloft and turned it in circles over my head. *"From sea to beach to solid ground, two worlds unite, what's lost is found; search the castle, take a peek, a selkie's skin is what we seek."*

We all looked around the room with wide eyes.

"Well, that was an utter failure," Hasenpfeffer said when nothing happened.

My shoulders slumped—I was so sure it would work.

Suddenly Hasenpfeffer gasped.

I turned just in time to see the bearskin rug from the tapestry room drop out of thin air on top of him.

"Ahhhhhh!" Hasenpfeffer shrieked. "Help! Somebody help me! I've been swallowed by a bear—it's digesting me as we speak. Oh, what a horrible way to go," he sobbed.

I quickly lifted the bear head up and exposed Hasenpfeffer. "It's just the rug—the same one you were lying on earlier."

Hasenpfeffer looked up and blinked. "Oh. So it is." He hopped slowly out from under the rug, with both ears dragging on the floor. "I hate Scotland," he muttered.

Mr. McGuire came rushing into the room. "Is everything all right? I heard screaming."

I looked guiltily at the bearskin in my hand. "Yes, everything's fine."

"Everything is *not* fine!" Fiona said. She walked up to

Mr. McGuire. "We were trying to find Mrs. Lachlan's and Lyra's sealskins, but the spell Maggie used didn't work and we got the bearskin rug instead."

"It almost killed me," Hasenpfeffer whimpered.

Mr. McGuire sighed as he took the bearskin rug from my hands. "Apparently Lyra wasn't the only one who heard Darcy's tale."

I nodded. "We heard the whole thing," I said. "Munro too."

Mr. McGuire snapped his suspenders. "This trip is not going at all as I'd hoped."

"Tell me about it," Hasenpfeffer said. He scratched his ears and then sat up. "I'm out of here. There's got to be someplace in this castle where a rabbit can rest in peace and quiet, and I'm going to find it." He scowled at us and then hopped out of the room.

"You'll help us, Mr. McGuire, won't you?" Fiona asked after Hasenpfeffer was gone. "You must know a spell that can locate the sealskins."

Mr. McGuire sat down on a couch and gestured for us to join him. "It's not that easy, I'm afraid," he said. "Sir Roderick confessed he doesn't know where the skins are."

I scoffed. "How could he not know? He's the one who hid them in the first place."

Mr. McGuire sighed. "That's true, he did, but the

spell he used to hide the pelts was cast in a moment of great duress. Lyra had just been born, and he panicked thinking he might someday lose both his wife and daughter to the sea. He said he used a powerful spell to hide the pelts in the castle and make them irretrievable; *then* he cast a spell so he'd forget where he'd put them—so he wouldn't change his mind."

"How could he do that to his own wife and child?" Fiona asked.

"Love does funny things to people," Mr. McGuire said. "Sometimes they make decisions that they live to regret, and Sir Roderick has expressed *deep* regret for what he did. And he tried to break the spell many, many times."

Fiona looked skeptically at Mr. McGuire. "But why would Mrs. Lachlan stay with him after what he did? I mean, that's not something a person could forgive easily."

Mr. McGuire nodded. "But she did. Not to say it's been an easy road for either one of them; sometimes love makes it easy to forgive—but not so easy to forget. Living in this castle knowing her sealskin was hidden, well, it's taken a toll on Rhona. And now Lyra." He hung his head, and I thought I'd never seen him look so tired and defeated. "We'll be leaving in the morning, though—the testing has been understandably canceled."

"That's it?" I said. "We're just going to give up and go home?"

Mr. McGuire nodded. "Unfortunately, Maggie, there are some spells that can't be broken. Sir Roderick has tried to find the pelts, but the spell he cast was too strong."

"But . . . ," I began.

"Maggie," Mr. McGuire said. "When we get home, we can do some research, okay? For now I think it's best if you all head off to bed. Mr. Shaw and I will be working with the mirror to make sure our journey home goes off without any problems. In the meantime, get some sleep."

"Wait, Mr. McGuire. What about the curse?" Fiona asked nervously. "Do you think it really could come true? Could we be in danger?"

Mr. McGuire shook his head. "These old stories are filled with halftruths and embellishments, and they change a little with each new telling. There have been many happy human-selkie marriages since Duncan Catherwood met his unfortunate end, so there is nothing to keep you from a good night's rest. Now off to bed."

An hour and a half later, Fiona and I stood in our room looking forlornly down at the bearskin rug sprawled out on my bed. "I give up!" I said. "I've lost count of how many spells we've tried, and all we keep getting is this *stupid* rug." I flicked my wand at it angrily and it vanished back to the tapestry room.

Fiona yawned. "We have to keep trying. Once we go home we won't be able to help them."

I flopped onto the bed and stared at the ceiling. "I think we just have to accept the fact that what Mr. McGuire said was true—the skins are irretrievable."

"Just because one magician can't break through a spell, doesn't mean another one couldn't, right?"

I sat up. "Maybe, but it's apparent that magician isn't me."

She walked to the dresser and started to unravel her braids. "We just have to try harder—think of new spell."

"Fiona, if Sir Roderick—the head of the Federation of Magic—can't figure out a way to break his own spell, what makes you think I can do it?"

Fiona turned from the mirror and folded her arms across her chest. "Because you said being smart doesn't mean you have to have a high IQ—or magic, for that matter. Maybe if we sleep on this, an answer will come to us in the morning. Hey, don't you think you should find Hasenpfeffer before we turn in?"

"No, he's probably found someplace 'quiet' to sleep, and I'll get an earful if I disturb his *beauty rest*."

As Fiona pulled a nightgown over her head, I looked

out the window. The storm had ended and a full moon shone brightly over the choppy sea. I could see seals bobbing in the moonlit surf. Could some of them be selkies? Could they be part of Mrs. Lachlan's family?

I knew how it felt to be separated from your family. I took a deep breath and wondered what my parents were doing right now. I hoped they missed me as much as I missed them. Even though coming to Bridgeport to stay with Gram had opened up this whole world of magic, casting spells didn't make up for going to bed every night without a kiss on the cheek from my mom and dad.

"It's too bad the walls can't talk," Fiona said as she pulled back the thick down comforter and slid into bed. "Because maybe they could tell us where Sir Roderick hid those skins."

My eyes widened. "Maybe they can!"

"What?" Fiona asked.

"What if there's a spell that *can* make walls talk?" I sat up in my bed. "We've been approaching this the wrong way. We need to act like this is a *repair job.*"

Fiona pumped her fist in the air. "Yes!"

"Mr. McGuire's got a whole shop full of books, and I bet one of them has the key to unlocking that spell. Since we're going home tomorrow, we can spend the whole day in the shop researching the spell, and when we find it, we can head back through the mirror and get those sealskins!"

Suddenly, a horrible, high-pitched scream pierced the air. Fiona and I jumped, our eyes wide and frightened.

"*No! Stay back!*" a voice wailed. "*Noooo!*"

"That's Hasenpfeffer!" I cried.

We leapt out of bed. I snatched my wand off the bureau and threw the door open. At the end of the hall was a large, black panther—with Hasenpfeffer dangling limply from its jaws. The panther growled, swished its tail, and then turned down the hall toward the staircase.

"Hasenpfeffer!" I screamed.

Raphael poked his head out of his room. "What's going on?" he asked sleepily. "Did I hear yelling?"

"A panther has Hasenpfeffer!" I called out as I raced after the big cat.

I reached the top of the stairs and saw the large wooden front door swing open. Mrs. Lachlan was coming in but leapt aside as the panther brushed past her into the night.

She put her hand to her chest and looked up at me as I thundered down the stairs. "Was that a wild cat?"

"Yes!" I said as I rushed past her to follow the creature.

"Maggie, no!" she cried. "Come back!"

I ignored her pleas, knowing I had to get to Hasenpfeffer before it was too late. I stood on the front lawn with my heart pounding and scanned the area. "Hasen-pfeffer!" I yelled. "Where are you?"

A low, guttural growl came from my right, and I ran around the side of the castle toward the noise. The large cat came into view poised on top of a wall, its fur gleaming in the moonlight. It growled again, and I took aim with my wand. *"Release!"* I screamed.

A red light flashed from the tip and hit the cat in the shoulder. Hasenpfeffer fell from its jaws as it let out an angry snarl and leapt out of sight on the other side of the wall.

I bolted down the lawn until I found Hasenpfeffer lying in the wet grass, his white fur soaked with dark blood. "No!"

His eyes fluttered opened for a second, and he groaned. "Maggie?" he whispered. "I don't feel so good. It's hard to breathe." He closed his eyes and a cough racked his body.

I gently scooped him up in my arms and choked back a sob. "Everything's going to be okay. Mr. McGuire will cast a spell and you'll be fine." My bottom lip quivered. "Everything is going to be fine."

Suddenly Mrs. Lachlan put an arm around me. "Hurry!" she said, leading me back toward the castle. "Bring him inside, and we'll see if Roderick can help."

When we reached the door, I saw Mr. McGuire,

Raphael, and Fiona standing in the front entryway.

Tears rolled down Fiona's cheeks when she saw Hasenpfeffer, and Raphael bowed his head. "Is he . . . ," Raphael began.

"He's alive, but just barely," I choked out. "Mr. McGuire, you have to do something," I sobbed.

He took Hasenpfeffer from my arms. "I'll try my best, Maggie. I'll bring him to Sir Roderick's workroom. I'm sure he'll have the ingredients I'll need."

I started to follow him, but Mrs. Lachlan put a hand on my arm. "I think it's best if you wait here."

"What is going on?" Darcy called out.

I looked up the stairs to see Darcy and her mother coming down in matching pink silk pajamas.

Mrs. Davenport had a sleeping mask pushed up on her forehead and was rubbing her temples. "Yes, what is all this ruckus about? I still have a splitting headache and really need my sleep."

"A *panther* attacked Hasenpfeffer in the castle," Fiona said.

Darcy gasped. "The curse—it came true!"

Mrs. Davenport swatted Darcy's shoulder. "I you told not to mention anything about that," she said through gritted teeth.

"Only she already did!" Raphael said angrily.

Mrs. Davenport stopped short on the stairs. "Darcy, you didn't!" she exclaimed.

Mrs. Lachlan stared coldly at Mrs. Davenport. "She did. She told Lyra of her selkie heritage—the knowledge of which is something I had chosen not to burden her with. I had hoped she wouldn't miss what she didn't know. But now . . ." Mrs. Lachlan glowered at Darcy, whose face flushed a fiery red. "Now I'm not sure we can ever mend the rift in our family."

"I'm sorry," Darcy said quietly. "Really I am. If I could take it all back, I would."

"Unfortunately for us, you can't. Now, if you'll excuse me," Mrs. Lachlan continued, "I'm going to fetch my husband so he can help Mr. McGuire attend to that poor creature, and then maybe we can figure out how a jungle cat appeared in the castle. You could make yourself useful, Delilah, and locate Ian—we will no doubt be in need of his assistance as well." She brushed past the Davenports and stomped up the stairs.

Mrs. Davenport turned on her daughter. "Darcy Eugenia Davenport! I repeatedly warned you to keep that information a secret! What possessed you to do such a thing?"

"I'm, I'm sorry, Mother," Darcy sputtered. "It just slipped out."

"*Just slipped out?*" Mrs. Davenport huffed. "And you didn't think to tell me?"

"You were asleep," she said quietly.

Mrs. Davenport threw her hands up in the air. "I'll tell you what else is out—my reputation! I told absolutely *everyone* that Sir Roderick was doing your testing, but now it would take a miracle to get him to do it. Do you know how humiliated I'm going to be?"

"One would think there were more important things to worry about, Delilah," Mr. Shaw said, walking into the entryway. "I would've surmised you'd be more concerned about how poor Lyra is fairing after hearing the devastating news she's a selkie."

"*Half* selkie," Darcy corrrected.

"For once in your life will you just shut up, Darcy?" Mrs. Davenport snapped. She turned back to Mr. Shaw. "*Of course* I'm concerned, Ian, and headache or no, I could kick myself for going to bed early and leaving Darcy unsupervised."

Mr. Shaw narrowed his eyes. "You and me both." He took a long drag on his pipe and blew a stream of bubbles up toward the ceiling.

"Mr. Shaw," I said with a quaking voice. "Mr. McGuire needs you. There was an attack: a panther—it got my rabbit. Mr. McGuire is trying to help him in Sir Roderick's workshop."

Mr. Shaw took the pipe out of his mouth and gasped. "Did you say 'panther'? In the castle?"

"It was huge," Raphael added.

Suddenly Mrs. Lachlan's screams were heard from upstairs. "No! No! Somebody help! Come quickly!"

"Rhona!" Mr. Shaw gasped.

We raced upstairs to see Mrs. Lachlan clinging to a doorway. "It's *Roderick!*" she cried. "He's been attacked. Oh, the blood! So much blood!" she wailed. Then her eyes rolled back into her head and Mr. Shaw swept her up in his arms as she lost consciousness and fell.

# 12

## Hanging by a Thread

aphael, Fiona, and I sat silently on the couches in the game room, waiting to hear news about Sir Roderick's and Hasenpfeffer's conditions. Darcy sat alone on the floor by the doorway, resting her head on her knees, which were drawn tightly to her chest. Spells had been cast around the room to protect us in case the panther reappeared.

I looked away from Darcy and tears welled up in my eyes as I pictured Hasenpfeffer lying on the grass with blood staining his snow white fur. "Why didn't I check on Hasenpfeffer when you asked where he was?" I said quietly to Fiona. "Maybe I would've seen the panther and could've warned everyone. Maybe I could've stopped it."

Raphael shook his head. "Or maybe it would have been you who . . ." He reached out and gave my hand a squeeze. "He'll be okay—and Sir Roderick, too. Mr. McGuire will know what to do."

I gave Raphael a halfsmile. "Thank you for not saying 'I told you so.' Apparently Mr. McGuire should've used more four-leaf clovers in his last spell, since I'm still attracting bad luck and dragging you along for the bumpy ride."

"At least things are never dull around you," he said.

I looked over at Darcy, and anger bubbled up inside me. I couldn't help thinking *she* was somehow responsible for what happened tonight. But then I noticed her shoulders quivering, and I realized she was crying.

I saw Fiona and Raphael gazing over at Darcy too.

"Should we say something to her?" Raphael whispered.

I shrugged, unsure what to do. It was Darcy's big mouth that started the nasty chain of events, but seeing *Darcy Davenport* curled into a ball—crying—made my stomach twist uncomfortably.

"Do you want to sit with us, Darcy?" Fiona said, as if reading my mind.

Darcy looked up—her face was red and blotchy and streaked with tears. She shook her head.

Fiona pointed to the embers glowing in the hearth. "It's warmer here by the fire."

Darcy scowled. "Like you really want me over there anyway."

The three of us exchanged a look. It was clear we *weren't* sure we did want her with us, but things had changed. People—and animals—had been hurt, and I honestly believed Darcy felt just as bad about it as we did.

"It really *is* warmer," I said.

Darcy stood up slowly and wiped her face with her sleeve. She jutted out her chin, walked over, and sat on the couch opposite us. "I'm sorry about your rabbit, Maggie."

"Thanks," I said.

"And I'm sorry about telling you all—*especially* Lyra—about . . ." Darcy stared off into the fire. "Sometimes I know I shouldn't say things, but the words leave my mouth anyway."

"You need to come to the repair shop—maybe we can fix that," I said.

Darcy nodded but refused to look at us. "Maybe."

Mr. McGuire walked into the room carrying a small box, and my heart froze. His face was pale and drawn.

"Hasenpfeffer?" was all I could choke out.

"He's hanging on," Mr. McGuire said as he placed the box on the coffee table. "But I won't lie to you. It's not good."

I shook my head in disbelief. "But we're magicians— there's got to be *something* to help him."

"Some things are bigger than magic," Mr. McGuire said. "And he's not responding to the usual healing spells. I'm sorry, Maggie, but you need to prepare for the worst."

"But he trusted me to take care of him . . ." I walked over to the table and looked into the box. The blood on Hasenpfeffer's fur had been mostly washed off, but traces of pink stained the area around his neck and the festering puncture wounds were clearly visible. I reached out and stroked his fur, feeling his chest move slowly with labored breaths. My face crumpled as a new wave of tears cascaded down. "I didn't do a very good job."

"Maggie." Mr. McGuire put an arm around my shoulders. "It's not your fault. There's just something about these wounds that won't let them heal; Sir Roderick's too. But with what's gone on, I need to get you all to Bridgeport as soon as possible. Help for Sir Roderick will arrive soon, and Mr. Shaw and I have stabilized the portal back to the repair shop. Let's gather our things, and then we can head home. Darcy, you're to wait here."

"Couldn't I please come with you?" Darcy asked solemnly. "I really don't think anyone wants me to stay here longer than I have to."

Mr. McGuire looked at her sympathetically. "I'm afraid not, Darcy. Though I offered my services, your mother wants to return through the photograph, but before you do, you'll need to be interviewed about exactly what you said regarding the shape-shifter's curse. It's possible you conjured up the panther accidentally."

Darcy shook her head. "I didn't, I swear! It *has* to be the curse."

Raphael scoffed. "The Lachlans have been married a long time; it would be *highly* coincidental that the curse would come to pass *right* after you told everyone about it. If you ask me, I'd say there's a better chance of an asteroid hitting the castle—and that's 182 trillion to one."

"I agree," Mr. McGuire said. "And since panthers aren't indigenous to Scotland, that means *someone* conjured it up."

"Well, it wasn't me!" Darcy declared. "Why would I cast a spell to bring a dangerous animal into the castle?"

Fiona eyed Darcy distrustfully. "Maybe you thought if it *looked* like the shape-shifter's curse had come true, everyone would be focused on that and not on what you did."

Darcy shook her head vigorously. "No! You have to believe me," she pleaded.

There was panic in Darcy's wide eyes, and I didn't

think she was worried about getting caught for something she'd done wrong—it looked like she was terrified of being accused of something she hadn't done.

"I believe you," I said. "But if Darcy didn't do it, someone else did—someone who didn't mind risking all of our lives." I looked around at everyone. "And that someone is still right here in the castle."

The doors leading to the outside opened, and we all jumped. Relief spread through me as Munro walked in instead of a wild cat.

"What's everyone still doing up?" he asked.

"What were *you* doing outside?" Mr. McGuire shot back suspiciously.

"I was looking for Lyra."

"Well, you're lucky you're unharmed; there's a panther loose on the grounds," Mr. McGuire said.

Munro looked quizzically at us. "Did you say 'panther'?"

I nodded. "Sir Roderick was hurt and . . ." I couldn't bring myself to say more.

Munro paled. "Have you seen Lyra? Do you know if she's okay?"

"I haven't seen her actually," Mr. McGuire said, his eyes filling with worry.

The rest of us shook our heads.

Munro took out his wand. "What if she's out there

with that creature?" Without another word, he bolted for the doors. "Lyra!" he screamed running out. *"Lyra!"*

I ran to Mr. McGuire. "Shouldn't we stop him?"

Mr. McGuire rushed over and shut the doors. "You and your friends are my top priority. I'll tell Ian—he'll go after him," he said breathlessly. "You hurry upstairs and fetch your things." He looked out into the night. "The sooner we leave Dark Craig Castle, the better."

I was the first one to step out of the mirror, and I smiled with relief to see the shop lit up and a familiar face standing in front of me—someone I was sure could help Hasenpfeffer. "Franny!" I cried.

I ran into her arms, and she hugged me tight. "Gregory called me and told me all about what happened and asked if I could lend a hand."

"Thank you for coming," Mr. McGuire said as he led Fiona and Raphael through the glass. "I feel terrible waking you at this hour."

I looked up at the large round clock hanging above the repair shop door and saw it was just after midnight.

"I wasn't asleep," Franny said, "but my new boyfriend was a little disappointed when I left him alone on the dance floor in the middle of a steamy tango—it takes two, after all."

"Sorry we interrupted you, but I'm so glad you're here," I said. "Franny works with magical animals—she's an expert," I told Fiona and Raphael, who were looking at her curiously. "I helped her with a repair job last week."

Franny shook her long, red curls away from her face and then patted her cheeks as if to be sure the blistering boils we cured her of were still gone. "And I'm *more* than happy to pay back the favor. Let me see the patient." She took the box with Hasenpfeffer nestled inside from Mr. McGuire and frowned as she peeked in. "Poor little guy," she said quietly.

She put the box on the counter. Hasenpfeffer moaned as she gently lifted him out and placed him on a thick towel she'd spread out. We gathered around as she ran her hands over his fur and examined his raw-looking wounds. "He's burning up with fever," she said. Then she reached into her purse and took out a shiny, green wand that was the same color as her eyes. She waved it over Hasenpfeffer and then clucked her tongue like Mr. McGuire does when he's thinking.

Franny looked at Mr. McGuire, and I held my breath waiting for her to announce that Hasenpfeffer was magically cured. Instead she just sighed. "Gregory, tell me exactly what happened again."

"I can tell you," I said before Mr. McGuire could answer. "Fiona and I heard a scream, and when we opened our bedroom door we saw . . ." My shoulders started to shake, and I couldn't get the words out.

"A *panther*," Fiona said. She put an arm around me, and I leaned into her, crying. "He had Hasenpfeffer in his mouth and ran outside with him."

Franny lifted Hasenpfeffer up and cradled him in her arms. She gently rocked him back and forth. "These wounds are *magic*," she said finally.

"Our best guess is that someone conjured the panther," Mr. McGuire said.

Franny shook her head. "No, not a panther."

"But I saw it!" I said. "So did Fiona and Mrs. Lachlan."

"What I mean to say is, it may have *looked* like a panther," Franny continued, "but whatever did this to Hasenpfeffer and Sir Lachlan was no ordinary cat. The fact that the wounds aren't responding to any spells points to a bite by a paranormal creature."

"Could a bite from a shape-shifter do it?" I asked.

"Perhaps," Franny said. "They're very powerful creatures. I know werewolves can pass on their lycanthropy to their victims, so it's very possible a different kind of shifter would have something dangerous about their bite—like nonhealing wounds."

Fiona turned to Franny. "Could a magician change into a panther?"

"He'd have to be very powerful, but it's possible," she replied.

Raphael's eyes widened. "So maybe someone at the castle, someone with a lot of power, took advantage of Darcy's story to get at Sir Roderick. Hasenpfeffer probably just got in the way."

"But who would do that?" Fiona asked.

I thought about the people who were at the castle with us. "What about Mr. Shaw?" I turned to Mr. McGuire. "Is it true he was in love with Mrs. Lachlan and that he tried to steal her way from Sir Roderick?"

"Well, yes," he replied, his cheeks flushing with embarrassment. "It was a bit messy, but that was years and years ago, and it was definitely one-sided. Rhona never encouraged him, and he and Sir Lachlan have patched up their friendship recently."

"Maybe that's what Mr. Shaw wants us to think," I said.

"And don't forget Mr. Shaw has that black cat," Raphael said. "Could he have transformed it into a panther? Hasenpfeffer had said the cat was watching him, and maybe after it attacked Sir Roderick it decided Hasenpfeffer was too good to pass up."

Mr. McGuire shook his head. "Transforming animals takes a lot of power. I confess I don't know the extent of

Ian's powers, but I've known him for years. I can't believe he'd do anything that would cause Rhona any pain—he loved her too much."

"Did he ever marry?" I asked.

Mr. McGuire pursed his lips. "No."

"Maybe seeing Mrs. Lachlan after all those years was too much for him," Fiona added. "Maybe he snapped. You even said love does funny things to people—makes them do things they'll regret."

Mr. McGuire brought a hand through his thin hair. "I don't want to believe it's true, but . . ."

"Hold on," Franny said. "Let's not jump to conclusions. Who else was at the castle?"

"Mr. Shaw's nephew Munro was there," I said, "and Mrs. Davenport and her daughter, Darcy."

"Delilah Davenport?" Franny asked.

I nodded.

"I know Delilah Davenport; she works for the MACPA with me—that's the Magical Animal, Plant, and Craft Association. We hold a fair every year, but I think we can rule her out as a suspect. She'd never do anything to smudge her spotless reputation—nothing so obvious, that is. But tell me about Munro."

"He's fifteen," I said. "And I think he has a crush on the Lachlans' daughter, Lyra."

"He's really cute," Fiona added. "And don't forget about Darcy. She was flirting like crazy with Munro. Maybe she did it to scare Munro away from Lyra."

"Darcy is *far* from perfect," I said, "but I can't shake the feeling she was genuinely upset about what happened."

"So that leaves Mr. Shaw and Munro," Raphael said. "And they each have a motive."

Fiona and I stared at Raphael. *"Munro?"*

Raphael nodded. "Munro was outside at the same time the panther was—it could have been him. He could've been trying to play the hero and find Lyra's sealskin."

"Tell me about the daughter, Lyra," Franny said.

I shook my head. "She got some bad news tonight. Darcy told her that she's part selkie—something her parents *hadn't* told her. She went off by herself."

Franny walked around the counter and sat on the seat. "Wow. That's news that would be hard to digest."

"But what about Hasenpfeffer?" I said. "Is there something you can do to help him?"

Franny looked down at my rabbit cradled in her arms. "We're going to need to do some research because right now I'm really not sure what to do. He's got an unknown poison flowing through him, and until we figure out what it is, I'm at a loss to help."

"Maybe I should take you kids to the apartment,"

Mr. McGuire said. He grimaced. "Your grandmother isn't going to like hearing about what happened, but I'd feel better if you were all tucked into some sleeping bags. Franny and I will get to work researching and see if we can come up with some answers."

I shook my head. "I'm not going anywhere until we find an answer."

"Same here," Fiona said.

"Me three," Raphael answered. "We'll have a better chance of helping Sir Roderick and Hasenpfeffer if we work together."

"I agree," Franny said. "Let them stay. We *have* to find an answer . . ." She looked down at Hasenpfeffer. "Fast."

Suddenly a familiar rattling came from a corner of the shop. We all turned and stared at Mr. McGuire's mailbox. Hot steam shot out, and the letters DD wavered and shimmered pink in the mist as the box let out a sharp whistle.

"It must be from Mrs. Davenport," I said. "Maybe there's news from the castle."

Mr. McGuire rushed over and opened the box. He waved away the steam and took out a pink flowered envelope. He ripped the envelope open and unfolded the letter. "Oh," he said looking up in surprise. "It's from Darcy."

# 13

## Darcy's Discovery

"**W**hat does it say?" I asked impatiently.

Mr. McGuire looked back to the letter and read it quickly. "It seems that while we've been talking suspects, Darcy has been doing research in one of her grandmother's books about shape-shifters." He turned to Franny. "You were right—the bite of a shape-shifter *does* carry venom with it, but an antidote can be made using the creature's blood."

Hasenpfeffer groaned weakly from Franny's arms.

"We have to get back to the castle and figure out who the shape-shifter is," I said. "Now!"

"Wait," Mr. McGuire said. "There's more. According to Darcy, if it is indeed a magician—"

"Like Mr. Shaw!" I interjected.

Mr. McGuire raised his eyebrows and cleared his throat. "They would have to be at least a level *ninety* to make the shift into animal form."

Franny's eyes widened as she let out a whistle. "You don't see that very often—like almost never."

"That rules out Darcy and her mom," Raphael said. "Darcy told us she was hoping to get a twenty-five on her test, which would be higher than anyone in her family."

"Munro told us he messed up a love potion and frequently uses magic dust number seven, which doesn't sound like a level ninety magician to me. It's got to be Mr. Shaw."

Mr. McGuire ran his hands up and down his suspenders. "I find it hard to believe he'd keep a number like that a secret. Ian was a bit of a braggart back in the day. But I can also imagine a magician of that power—a sorcerer to be precise—might want to keep that information secret."

I pointed toward the mirror. "There's only one way to find out. We have to go back to Scotland."

Mr. McGuire folded his arms across his chest and shook his head. "Maggie, you know I can't bring you back. Your grandmother would never speak to me again."

I sighed dramatically. "I know," I said forlornly. "You go with Franny and Hasenpfeffer, and we'll wait here. The important thing is that Sir Roderick and Hasenpfeffer get better. And while you're gone I'll write to Viola Klemp and see if she can get a copy of Mr. Shaw's license."

Raphael eyed me suspiciously, and I gave him a look I hoped would convey that we shouldn't argue with Mr. McGuire.

"Yeeeeeah," Raphael said, drawing out the word as he caught on. "I wouldn't want to mess around with that panther again. I mean, two wild cats in less than a week is two too many."

"Two!" Fiona exclaimed.

I wrinkled my nose. "Did I forget to mention the lion in the shop last week?"

Fiona looked around nervously. "Yes, you forgot to mention that."

Franny stood up and placed Hasenpfeffer gently back in the box. "We should go, Gregory. The longer we wait . . ."

"All right," Mr. McGuire said. "You kids wait here, and I'll send an update as soon as possible."

"Wait! How do I work the mailbox?" I asked.

Mr. McGuire hurried behind the counter and took out some paper and an envelope. "Write Viola and ask her for a copy of Mr. Shaw's license." He paused. "But don't tell her why we need it—make something up. The less she knows about what happened this evening, the better. When you're done, place the envelope in the mailbox and pour a cup of water in with it."

I looked back and forth between the mailbox and Mr. McGuire. *"Water?"*

"Yes." He scribbled on a piece of paper and handed it to me. "Once you shut the box, put the red flag up, and then tap it with your wand. Recite this spell and the vapor will break up the letter. It will reform in a box at Viola's house."

"Got it," I said.

Hasenpfeffer let out a pained wheeze, and Franny bit her lip, obviously worried. "Let's hurry, Gregory."

Mr. McGuire walked up to me, put a hand on each of my shoulders, and stared right into my eyes. "You-are-*not*-to-leave-this-shop! Understood?"

I held my hand up like I was taking an oath. "Understood! We're going to wait to hear from Viola, and if we get a copy of the license, we'll send it to the castle via mailbox."

"Good!" he said. "Let's go, Franny."

I watched them leave through the mirror, and then ran to the counter. I snatched up a pen. "Get some water,

Fiona!" I jotted a quick note to Viola, stuffed it in the envelope, and shoved it into the box. Fiona handed me a cup of water, and I tossed it in and slammed the door shut. I lifted the flag and took out my wand and read the spell Mr. McGuire had left. *"Send a letter, RSVP, Viola to Maggie, quick as can be; the news it seems is boiling hot, alert the recipient like a whistling pot."* I tapped the mailbox with my wand and steam shot through the crack in the door.

I turned to Raphael and Fiona. "As soon as we get a response we'll head back through the mirror to Scotland."

Raphael threw his hands up in the air. "I *knew* you were going to say that."

"I didn't!" Fiona exclaimed.

Raphael rolled his eyes at her. "Maggie has *major* problems following directions."

"Hasenpfeffer is over there—hurt. I need to be with him."

Fiona nodded. "I'm with you to the end."

Raphael stared bug-eyed at us. "Do you girls have a death wish built into your DNA? I'm already having nightmares about being eaten by a lion—I don't want to add a panther to the mix."

I folded my arms across my chest. "What if it was *Pip* at the castle?"

Raphael hung his head. "Nothing could keep me

away," he said finally. He looked up. "If we do hear from Viola, I'll go."

We all turned to look at the mailbox.

Nothing.

"What if she's asleep?" I said, rapping my fingers impatiently on the counter. "What if she doesn't get the letter until morning, and by then it's too late?"

Fiona tapped her ear. "That whistle was pretty loud. I think she'd hear it."

Raphael nodded in agreement. "And I bet an old busybody like Viola Klemp has mailboxes all over her house—probably one right next to her bed so she doesn't miss anything."

The mailbox rattled and we all cringed as an ear-piercing whistle rang out. Within the steam pouring out of the box, the letters vk appeared.

Raphael smirked. "Told you so."

My hand burned in the hot vapor as I grabbed the envelope out of the mailbox, shoved my finger under the hot wax seal, and tore open the back flap. I took the letter out and my shoulders slumped as I looked at the numbers listed. "It's *not* Mr. Shaw—not by a long shot. But look at Sir Roderick's number. He's a level *seventy-nine!*"

I held the letter out, and Raphael and Fiona read through it quickly.

"Why did you ask Viola for Sir Roderick's numbers?" Raphael asked. "It's not like he could've attacked himself."

I shrugged. "I don't know. I just had a feeling we needed to cover all of our bases."

Fiona sighed. "Now we're back at the beginning, with *no* suspects. There were a lot of servants working at the castle—it could be any of them."

"It's possible." I shook my head. "Wait! We *haven't* covered all of our bases—we forgot to take into account one *very* important person. Someone whose world was just turned completely upside down and maybe wasn't thinking clearly."

Fiona's eyes widened. "Lyra? I didn't even think she *was* a magician—I didn't see her casting any spells, and she didn't play Zap so I just assumed . . ."

"Me too," I said. "That's why I didn't suspect she could've been behind the attack. When she came in from the storm, Munro fussed over her like she wouldn't have been able to light the fire or dry her own clothes with a spell—but that doesn't mean she *couldn't*. Do you remember what Darcy said about the selkies?"

Raphael's mouth formed a large O. "Yes! Selkies have 'mysterious magic as old and powerful as the oceans.' If you combine Mr. and Mrs. Lachlan's powers, Lyra's magic is probably off the charts!"

"But why would she do it?" Fiona asked. "I know she was upset, but how could she have attacked her own father?"

"Only Lyra can answer that question," I said. "Let's get to the castle and tell them what really happened so we can save Sir Roderick and Hasenpfeffer!"

I leapt out of the mirror to find shouts and accusations echoing around the tapestry room. Mr. Shaw was arguing loudly with Mr. McGuire and Franny, while Mrs. Lachlan was pleading with them to stop fighting and help her find Lyra.

I ran up to Mr. McGuire and handed him the letter. "It's not Mr. Shaw! It couldn't be."

The room quieted as Mr. McGuire looked at Viola's message.

"He doesn't have the power to turn a grasshopper into an ant," I said.

Mr. Shaw raised an eyebrow as his cheeks burned brightly. "My powers, or lack thereof, are a closely guarded secret!" He blew a series of bubbles with his pipe. "Besides, as I was trying to tell Gregory, you'd be hard-pressed to find a magician with the power needed for this sort transformation. Outside werewolfism, it's practically unheard of!"

"Until now," Raphael said. "Lyra could do it."

"That's nonsense," Mrs. Lachlan declared. "You can't seriously be suggesting Lyra attacked Roderick? She hardly even uses magic. She says she doesn't feel the need."

Mr. McGuire grasped his suspenders with one hand. "Maybe *that's* the problem. Being inexperienced, she could've bitten off more than she could chew." He grimaced. "Sorry, poor choice of words."

"If she can't control herself, she's in danger too," Franny said.

"You have to help me find her!" Mrs. Lachlan implored.

The next moment, Munro walked in carrying Lyra in his arms. She clung to his neck, weeping. He gently laid her down on one of the couches by the fire, and her mother rushed to her and brushed aside her matted, tangled hair.

Mrs. Lachlan gasped. "Lyra, are you all right?"

She turned to her mother with red-rimmed eyes. "I'm sorry—so very sorry. I was only trying to help you."

Mrs. Lachlan took one of Lyra's hands, and I saw it was covered with what looked like dried blood. Lyra buried her face in her mother's chest and sobbed. "I thought if Father believed the curse was coming true, he'd find a way to give you your sealskin back. I found a spell in one of his books. I didn't know if it would even work—I wasn't sure I had the power—but when I transformed, the instincts of the cat were too strong. I tried to keep in control, but I couldn't. It was only upon hearing Munro call for me that I was able to remember who I was and shed the form of the panther."

Mrs. Lachlan hugged her daughter. "Oh, my poor darling."

"I only wanted you to be happy, Mother. I wanted you to be able to return to your family."

"Oh, but you *are* my family," Mrs. Lachlan said. "You and your father, and I wouldn't trade either one of you for anything."

"You must hate me for what I've done!" Lyra cried.

Mrs. Lachlan hugged her furiously. "No, darling, no!"

"Nor I," Munro said softly as he sat down and gently stroked her hair.

"Is Father . . ."

"Your father will be all right if we move quickly," Mr. McGuire said. "We need to get Lyra to the workroom to concoct the antidote. Darcy sent the ingredient list, so we shouldn't have any trouble, but time is of the essence."

Munro scooped Lyra up in his arms. "Wait," she whispered. She turned her head to me. "I'm sorry," she said breathlessly. "So very sorry."

I nodded and Munro swept her out of the room. Mrs. Lachlan, Mr. McGuire, and Franny hurried after them, and I was left alone with Fiona and Raphael.

I plopped down on the couch and sank back into the pillows as the weight of what had happened and the lack of sleep made of my limbs feel as if they were each a hundred pounds.

Raphael and Fiona sat down on the couch opposite me, yawning.

"Well that's it, then," Raphael said. "They'll make up the antidote and fix Sir Roderick and Hasenpfeffer."

I rubbed my eyes. "And when I see him, I'm going to magic him up the biggest bowl of parsley he's ever seen. And maybe I'll get him a poster of Japan to hang in my room."

"Japan?" Fiona asked wearily.

I smiled. "Apparently Milo and Hasenpfeffer were *very* big in Japan. He talks about it all of the time. Unfortunately he's stuck with me in Bridgeport, forced to lead a decidedly nonglamorous life."

"He'll realize how lucky he is to have you," Fiona said. She yawned again. "He probably just needs time to get used to the idea."

I nodded, and the next thing I knew, someone was lightly shaking one of my shoulders.

"Maggie, wake up," a voice whispered.

I opened my eyes and saw Franny kneeling down in front of me. "Is Hasenpfeffer here?" I asked, looking past her expecting to see him hopping around the room, but all I saw was Raphael and Fiona slumped on the other couch, snoring softly.

Franny bit her lip and shook her head. "No, honey. He's not responding to the antidote."

I sat up, my heart crashing against my chest. *"What do you mean?"*

She lowered herself onto the couch next to me. "It's just that he's so small, and there was a lot of venom coursing through his veins. If we had gotten to him a little sooner. . . ."

"He's not . . ."

"No, he's trying to hang on. He's a tough little guy. We shouldn't move him, though, so I'm going to stay here while Gregory brings you back home."

I stood up. "I'm not leaving him!"

Franny put a finger onto her lips and tilted her head toward Raphael and Fiona. She took my hand and pulled me gently back down to the couch. "The Lachlans have a lot to deal with without a bunch of extra guests. You go back, and I promise to keep you updated." She gave me a small smile. "I even have a cell phone so we don't need to use an old-fashioned mailbox."

Tears stung my eyes. "Can I see him before I go?"

She nodded and led me out of the room. We walked down a long corridor in silence and then turned into a workroom that reminded me of Mr. McGuire's shop, only ten times bigger. A cauldron simmered in an oversize fireplace. Books were stacked floor to ceiling on shelves, and in a corner Mr. McGuire sat holding Hasenpfeffer wrapped up in a pink blanket.

"He *hates* pink," I said, before dissolving into tears. I held my arms out, and Mr. McGuire slowly transferred Hasenpfeffer to me, and then helped me into the chair. I stroked Hasenpfeffer's ears, alarmed at how hot they felt.

"I can't make any promises," Franny said. "But I'll do everything I can."

"You'd better get well," I whispered into Hasenpfeffer's ears. "I heard Gram say she was buying a new lamp, and I know you're going to want to chew the cord. I'm redecorating my room too—no more unicorns. I think a sophisticated traveler such as yourself will like what I have in mind, but you need to get well so you can see it."

Mr. McGuire cleared his throat. "We should be getting home now."

"I *wish* you'd get better," I said, hoping a little extra magic might help him. I kissed Hasenpfeffer on the top of his head and reluctantly gave him to Franny.

Mr. McGuire sighed. "I'm not looking forward to telling your grandmother about what's happened, but hope-fully she'll understand. Who could have predicted we'd encounter such a mess at the home of the chairperson of the World Federation of Magic?"

I shook my head. Gram was just getting used to the idea of me being a magician and working in the shop—how would she feel when she discovered I'd just had another magical close call?

# 14

## Needle in a Haystack

"Girls," Gram said, knocking on my bedroom door. "It's late—why don't you get up?"

I groaned and rubbed my eyes. I rolled over and saw Fiona was just starting to stir in her sleeping bag on my floor.

"What time is it?" she asked sleepily.

"One thirty!" I said, squinting at my clock. "We slept through lunch."

We'd arrived at my apartment at four in the morning, and to say Gram was surprised to see Fiona and Raphael with me would be an understatement. She and

Mr. McGuire had a heated discussion about what to do with them. Gram made it clear she didn't like the idea of them staying over without their parents' knowledge, but when Fiona suggested Mr. McGuire drop them off at the retreat and cast another memory spell, Gram agreed to let them sleep over. The plan was to have Gram call their parents to say she'd pick them up from the retreat so we could work on a school project. That way they'd never know Fiona and Raphael weren't where they were supposed to be.

We had gotten Raphael set up with pillows and blankets on the couch, and as Fiona and I headed to my room, I heard Mr. McGuire start to tell Gram about everything that had happened. The last thing I heard before I shut my door was Gram gasp and say, "Hasenpfeffer? Oh no, the poor thing."

I couldn't help smiling knowing that Gram liked Hasenpfeffer more than she let on.

Fiona stood up and shook out her hair. "We should get to the shop as soon as possible. I was hoping we were going to get an earlier start."

"The shop?" I asked.

Fiona picked my brush up off my dresser and ran it through her hair. She parted it down the back and began to braid one side. "We can't very well research a spell to find the sealskins from your apartment."

"Fiona, I don't think my grandmother is going to let us even go to the shop."

She looked at me quizzically. "Why wouldn't she? Don't you think she'd want us to help the Lachlans?"

"I don't know, but I do know she wouldn't want to risk having someone see you two walking in the street. Raphael lives right above us—it would be too risky."

Fiona tugged on her braids. "We'll put on a disguise."

I shook my head. "Disguise or no, there's no way you're going to convince my grandmother. You don't know her like I do."

"Well, it won't hurt to ask, right?"

I shrugged. "Ask away, but I'd bet money we're spending the rest of today holed up in the apartment."

I stared at Gram as Fiona explained why it was imperative she let us go to the shop. She was listening to Fiona intently, nodding her head, and nibbling the brownish red lipstick off her bottom lip. I was still having trouble adjusting to this "new" Gram—one who was okay with magic. I had been expecting Gram to huff and puff about why we couldn't go, and instead she was giving Fiona her undivided attention.

"So you see why we have to find a spell," Fiona said solemnly. "Can you imagine magic keeping you from being who you truly are? Keeping you from part of your family?"

Gram walked to the window. She parted the curtains and looked out. Her shoulders slumped as she let out a long sigh. "No," she said. "I can't."

Fiona and I exchanged a look. "Told you so," she whispered.

Gram turned to us. "I have hats and shawls and things you can put on so no one will recognize you—"

"You're going to let us go?" I asked. *Really?*

Gram nodded. "As much as I enjoyed my visit with Mrs. Lachlan at the castle, I couldn't shake the feeling she was filled with great sadness. If it's within your ability to help her and Lyra, I will give you my full support. But I insist you have something to eat first."

Fiona beamed. "I'll help make sandwiches, and then we can go!"

A s we approached the shop I saw a familiar blue, daisy-covered van parked out front. "It's Mr. Fishbone," I said.

Raphael pulled down the oversize sunglasses he was wearing. "Who's Mr. Fishbone?"

"Clarence Fishbone. Mr. McGuire and I did a job for him last weekend. He brought in his rabbit . . ." I inhaled sharply. We hadn't gotten an update about Hasenpfeffer for hours.

Fiona squeezed my arm. "Maybe Mr. McGuire has some news."

I nodded and we all rushed down the stairs to the shop. Raphael opened the door, and I saw Mr. McGuire measuring out a good helping of magic dust number seven into a jar and Mr. Fishbone wearing faded blue jeans and a red plaid flannel shirt instead of his clown outfit.

Mr. Fishbone turned and clasped his hands to his chest when he saw me. "Oh, I'm so sorry to hear about your little bunny. Breaks me heart it does. Can't imagine what I'd do if it were my Gertrude in the same situation."

"Thanks," I said.

Mr. Fishbone let out a whistle. "It's hard to believe what went on at that castle," he continued. "*Everyone's* buzzing about it."

Mr. McGuire cleared his throat. "Now, Clarence, we mustn't gossip."

Mr. Fishbone scoffed. "When the chairman of the Federation of Magic is almost killed by his own child taking the form of a beast, it's not gossip; it's news, it is! You just concern yourself with measuring out me magic dust so I can make some more money to pay you back."

Mr. McGuire rolled his eyes

Fiona walked up to Clarence. "Hello, Mr. Fishbone. I'm Fiona Fitzgerald. Do you know anything about breaking irretrievable spells?"

Mr. Fishbone laughed. "I'm a *party* magician, little missy; I don't know nothing about such things. That's what Gregory is for. But . . ." He ducked his head and leaned in close to me. "I have something to tell you. Remember that spell I showed you—the one with the dog?"

"Yes."

He grinned from ear to ear. "It's part of me act now. I told the wife we needed to change things up so I could be bringing in some money." He stood up proudly. "I'm booked for three solid months, I am! I send every kid home with a barking balloon. I fixed it so they don't last but a day and told the kids it's done with computer chips."

He laughed. "The kids and their parents flipped for them pooches, and everyone wants me for their party now. Of course, if Viola Klemp knew what I was up to she'd have a right cow, wouldn't she?"

"She just might," I said.

Clarence puffed out his chest and waved his hand in the air dismissively. "I'm not afraid of the likes of Viola Klemp. I heard what Sir Roderick thinks about her, and if the chairman of the Federation of Magic said she's a right busybody, who am I to disagree?"

I cringed. "That's not *exactly* what he said." Viola Klemp's reputation had apparently taken a hit this weekend, and I could only imagine how Sir Roderick's words would get further twisted as the news spread. I wondered if Mrs. Davenport was behind the rumor mill. I could imagine her trash-talking Viola in an attempt to downplay Darcy's involvement in what had happened.

"Are you sure you don't know anything about irretrievable spells?" Fiona asked.

Clarence shook his head. "But I can make you a nifty little pup if you want!" He bent over to his suitcase to get a balloon.

"No thanks," Raphael said. "We have work to do."

Clarence straightened up and looked at Raphael. "You're the kind of kid that's making it hard for us party magicians—no time for fun."

"Here's your magic dust," Mr. McGuire said, handing Mr. Fishbone a brown paper bag. Make sure you keep it safely tucked away in your suitcase so Gertrude's flying act doesn't get out of hand again."

Mr. Fishbone winked. "I cast a spell so the magic dust is hidden in plain sight right here in me case. Any nosy kid poking around in me things will think he's stumbled upon my denture cream." He smiled wide, showing off his false teeth.

"Hey, I just thought of something," I said. "Maybe we shouldn't be trying to *retrieve* the skins—maybe we should be trying to find out where they're *hidden*."

"But finding a hiding place in a castle," Raphael said, "is like finding a needle in a haystack. There are probably a million places you could stash something—and knowing magic is involved, the skins could be in the walls or hidden under the floor."

Mr. Fishbone scratched his head. "You know what I would do, if I had the power?"

We looked at him with anticipation.

"I'd shrink myself to the size of a mouse. That ways I could reach all the nooks and crannies a big person couldn't."

Raphael furrowed his brow. "But it would take forever for a mini-you to search a castle; statistically speaking it would be easier to—" He stopped when he saw Mr. Fishbone looking embarrassed.

Mr. Fishbone shrugged. "It was a silly idea."

"No," I said, glaring at Raphael. "It was a great idea. A mini-you *could* search behind the walls. And what better place to hide something?"

He gave me a small smile. "I best be heading off. I have

a party this evening, and I've got to iron me clown suit."

"I hope you have a good show, Clarence," Mr. McGuire said.

"Thanks! And thanks for the magic dust. I'll be seeing you soon to finish paying off me bill."

When Mr. Fishbone left, we started grilling Mr. McGuire about potential spells to find the selkie skins.

"We were thinking maybe about a spell that could make the walls talk," I started. "That way they could tell us where the pelts are hidden."

Mr. McGuire nodded appreciatively. "That's a clever idea, and there are spells that allow inanimate objects talk, but I've never heard of a spell that could get such an object to *think*."

"What's the difference?" Fiona asked.

"In order for the walls to truly tell us anything of value, they'd need to be self-aware. For instance, I saw a large statue of a French poodle that someone had enchanted to sing the alphabet like an opera star."

Raphael laughed. "That could get old fast!"

"Yes," Mr. McGuire continued, "but the dog didn't choose to sing that particular song; it couldn't think for itself. I think you may be attacking this job from the right angle, though. By concentrating on a spell to *reveal* the location of the seal pelts as opposed to trying to magically *retrieve* them, we might stumble on something that will work."

He clucked his tongue as he walked over to the bookshelves and looked at the titles. "Try looking through this one," he said, reaching for a small, black book *"Unbreakable,"* he said. "It has tips for dealing with seemingly unbreakable spells." He gave me the book and then walked along the shelves some more. "This could be helpful," he said, pulling out a thick, brown book and placing it on the counter. *"Search and Rescue: Spells for Finding Lost Objects, People, and Pets."*

I sighed. "Pets."

"Maybe we can look for a spell that might help Hasenpfeffer too," Fiona said.

Mr. McGuire smiled. "I was doing just that before Clarence arrived. I borrowed a book on shape-shifters to see if I can find information on venomous bites. No luck as of yet, but I know Franny is also doing research in Sir Roderick's extensive library."

"That's good to know," I said.

Fiona took the book off the counter. "I'll take *Search and Rescue.*"

"I'll look on the shelves some more, Mr. McGuire," Raphael said, "so you can keep reading."

Mr. McGuire nodded and then folded his arms across

his chest. "Before you get started, I want to say that as much as I appreciate the fact that you all want to help the Lachlans, you need to know that breaking his spell will be difficult to near impossible. Some books assign a power ranking to their spells, so be mindful that Sir Roderick is a level seventy-nine. Because of the power behind the spells he used to hide the skins and protect them from detection, it's likely only Sir Roderick will be able to make the actual repair."

"If we do find a spell, do you think Sir Roderick would actually try it?" I asked.

"I *know* he would," Mr. McGuire said. "Before the attack, he had already promised to renew his search for the pelts."

I opened *Unbreakable*. "Let's get started!"

By the time Gram called the shop a few hours later to announce dinner would be ready soon, we'd come up only with three potential spells for Sir Roderick to try. One was in *Search and Rescue*, one in a book Fiona found about uncovering hidden objects like leprechaun gold and pirate's treasure, and a third Raphael read about in a book written by an Aborigine magician.

"I'll get these to Sir Roderick right away," Mr. McGuire said.

Fiona squealed with joy and high-fived Raphael.

I held my hand up too, but I had a feeling none of these spells would successfully uncover the pelts.

Raphael placed the large sunglasses on his head and pulled my grandfather's old ball cap low on his forehead. "I wish there was a place to find the statistics for breaking a spell," he said.

Fiona put on Gram's wide-brimmed bonnet and wrapped a scarf around her neck. "You'll let us know if one of them works, right, Mr. McGuire?"

"Absolutely." He peered out the storefront window and then checked his watch. "It's late; let me accompany you back to the apartment."

I looked in his eyes and could tell he was also doubtful these spells would work. As we walked up the steps to the sidewalk I couldn't help thinking the spell we needed wasn't going to be found in any book.

"Mrs. Lachlan might be able to return to her family soon!" Fiona gushed. "I'm going to cross my fingers all the way back to your apartment."

Raphael flung his arm out in front of him like he was throwing a Frisbee. "I'm thinking the one using the boomerang to reverse spells as it doubles back has a pretty good shot."

"Yeah," I said halfheartedly.

I looked up at the darkening sky.

How do you retrieve the irretrievable?

How do you uncover what's been magically hidden?

I shook my head because another thought had just crept into my mind. As much as I believed Sir Roderick was truly sorry about what he'd done, I wondered if a part of him was scared that if he returned the pelts, he'd never see Mrs. Lachlan and Lyra again.

Could doubt affect the success of a spell? Could that be why, despite all of his efforts, he'd never been able to break the spells he cast?

If that were true, someone else would have to do it.

# 15

## All Creatures, Great and Small

ram knocked on my bedroom door Monday morning, and I rolled over and pulled my pillow over my head. I hoped she wouldn't force me to go to school. I wanted to stay home in case there was an update about Hasenpfeffer.

"Maggie?" Gram called out. "Can I come in?"

Without waiting for me to answer, Gram opened the door. The floorboards creaked as she crossed the room, and I felt her weight shift the mattress as she sat down on my bed.

"Would you like to see what I made?" she asked.

I shook my head under the pillow. "No" was my muffled reply.

Gram took my pillow off and I sighed. "Fine. What?"

I slowly sat up and saw Gram holding a sign that read WELCOME HOME, HASENPFEFFER! LOVE, MAGGIE AND GRAM," rendered in bright markers.

My eyes widened. "He's coming home? Did you hear from Franny?"

Gram put a hand to her chest. "No. I didn't mean to mislead you, but I thought we needed to think positively about the situation."

My bottom lip quivered and I leaned in and hugged Gram tight. "But what if he *doesn't* come home?"

Gram gently pushed me back. "Knowing that rabbit like we do, can you really doubt he won't be back to pester us with his never-ending prattle?"

"But there's been no word from the castle."

"Franny called while you were asleep," Gram said. "There's been no change. She also wanted to let you know that Sir Roderick tried the spells from the list you sent him—he didn't have any luck."

"I'm not surprised," I said softly.

Gram stood up and placed the poster on my desk. "You hang this up in anticipation of Hasenpfeffer's return and get ready for school."

"Couldn't I stay here—just for today—in case he comes home?"

"You need to be around people, Maggie, not moping in your room. I know you're hurting, but we have to keep on living." Gram hung her head. "We have to keep on living no matter how hard it hurts." She cleared her throat. "I'll pack your lunch," she said as she hurried out my door.

"*Gram!*" I called out.

She peeked her head back in my room.

"Thank you," I said, "for the poster, and thanks for letting Raphael and Fiona stay over."

Gram put her hands on her hips. "I didn't have much choice about that, not with Mr. McGuire bringing you back after four in the morning!" She sighed. "It's like living with your father all over again."

Her eyes widened as if she couldn't believe what had just come out of her mouth. "What I, uh, I mean is he was always having sleepovers." She nodded and then pointed down the hall. "I'd better get that lunch going so you won't miss your bus."

Gram's hurried footsteps echoed down the hall as she made her way toward the kitchen. I slid my legs out from under my covers and walked over to my desk, picking up the poster and marveling that Gram had taken the time to make it.

*But what if I hang this up and Hasenpfeffer doesn't come home?* I asked myself.

I shook my head. *Think positively!* I took out some tacks and put the poster up over my computer where Hasenpfeffer would be able to see it from his cage.

"Come home soon," I whispered.

Raphael wasn't on the bus that morning so I spent the ride to school making wishes Hasenpfeffer would get better. When I walked into the classroom, I saw Sal and Max playing chess, and Serena and Nahla were spraying paint on the canvas Ms. Wiggins had started last week. Darcy was at her desk, and Fiona was sitting with a book in her lap in the reading corner.

"Maggie!" Ms. Wiggins called out, rushing toward to me. She was wearing a long, flowing brown dress and had a circlet adorned with tiny bells tied around her head that jingled as she walked. She clasped her hands under her chin, smiling. "I hope you had a delightful visit with your uncle from Scotland. I know how utterly *devastated* you were to drop out of the retreat, so I have something for you and Darcy."

She tilted her head in Darcy's direction. "The poor thing took ill and was also not able to make our rejuvenating sojourn." She paused and looked around the room.

"And if anyone needed a relaxing meditative retreat, it was our Darcy," she whispered.

She looked down at me in surprise. "Oh, let's just keep that last bit to ourselves, shall we?"

I nodded, and Ms. Wiggins smiled as she led me over to Darcy, who was staring intently at a laptop computer open on her desk.

"Darcy," Ms. Wiggins began. "Since you and Maggie were unable to join us this weekend, I bought you each a little something."

Darcy looked up and stared blankly at Ms. Wiggins. I tried to read Darcy's expression, but she seemed all business this morning, like what had happened in Scotland was a million years in the past.

"You won't believe this," Ms. Wiggins continued, "but I discovered the Mongolian Songstresses have just released a new CD inspired by *sheep!*" She shook her balled-up hands by her sides and squealed as if this were earth-shattering news. "And . . ." Ms. Wiggins fumbled through an oversize pocket on her dress and pulled out two CDs. "I bought you each a copy!"

The cover of the CD showed an Asian woman playing some sort of wind instrument in a meadow with a line of sheep trailing after her. "Thank you." I scrambled to come up with something else Ms. Wiggins would appreciate.

"This will *surely* help me find my . . . *inner nomad* and . . ." My mind raced. "And help ground me for this year's many difficult tasks."

Ms. Wiggins beamed. "Spoken like a true kindred spirit!"

Darcy gave Ms. Wiggins a pained smile. "Who doesn't like music inspired by *sheep*?"

"Exactly! And perhaps the music will help inspire you as you continue to work on your weaving, Ms. Davenport. You seem to be lagging behind everyone else."

"Ms. Wiggins!" Nahla called out. "Serena sprayed me with paint!"

"It was an accident," Serena insisted.

"It was not," Nahla complained.

"Girls, art is supposed to be soothing, not combative!" Ms. Wiggins said as she raced off toward them.

"How's your rabbit?" Darcy asked.

"Not good."

She sat up in her chair with a furrowed brow. "I thought once the antidote was made he'd be okay."

I sighed. "So did I."

"I hope he gets better."

Fiona came over to us, her eyes wide and hopeful. "How's Hasenpfeffer?" she whispered.

I shook my head. "No change."

"Oh," she said, looking disappointed. "What about the spells? Did Sir Roderick try them yet?"

"What spells?" Darcy asked.

Fiona got that hopeful look on her face again. "We spent time in the repair shop researching spells that might find the sealskins. We found three that we thought just might work."

"You're still worrying about *that*?" Darcy asked in amazement. "I'd be more worried about your speech today."

"Speech?" Fiona gulped as her faced flushed. "That's today?"

A snaky smile broke out on Darcy's face. "You didn't write your election speech?"

"No. I was planning on composing it in my head at the retreat. But I've been so worried about Hasenpfeffer and the Lachlans that I completely forgot about it."

"That's too bad," Darcy said with fake sincerity. "I was just going over my speech and PowerPoint presentation, but I'm sure you'll be able to wing it." She stood up and got in close to my face. "And by the way, I know you cast some sort of spell to make everyone think Fiona would make the *perfect* president, so you'd better undo it or I'm telling my mother. I plan on winning because I'm the better candidate, and if everyone votes for Fiona, we'll both know the election was rigged."

"That's fine," I said. "Fiona doesn't need any magical help to win."

"Yeah," Fiona said, but she didn't look like she believed that was true.

Darcy shook her head and looked at us like we were crazy. "She doesn't even have a *speech*. I know you two are new here, but we take this pretty seriously."

"I think you're the only one who takes it seriously," I said. "Everyone else is happy taking turns in the election."

Darcy stood tall. "Well, I'm not everyone, and I know what the other kids are looking for in a class president."

Fiona paled. "May the best person win," she said quietly.

Ms. Wiggins clapped her hands. "Class! It's time for our morning meeting."

Darcy stalked off toward the rug, and I rolled my eyes. "Don't worry about the speech. Just say whatever comes to mind, and I'm sure it'll be hundred percent better than whatever Darcy has planned."

"I hope so," Fiona said. "Darcy certainly has a lot more in common with everyone, though—and they've known her for years."

"Don't forget, just because you and I are different doesn't mean we can't compete with them. You can count on my vote; Raphael's too if he gets here." I looked around. "Where could he be?"

"Girls!" Ms. Wiggins called out.

Fiona and I took our seats on the rug and Ms. Wiggins unwrapped the talking stick. "First, I want each of you to share a special memory of our weekend together, and let's ask the universe to ensure Darcy and Maggie will be able to join us next year. Sal, will you start off?"

Sal took the stick with a little grimace. "Um, I liked the cheese they gave us this year."

Giggles erupted around us.

"Well, it was better than the stuff we got last year," he insisted.

"I was hoping you'd dig deeper, Sal," Ms. Wiggins said. *"Dig into your soul."*

Sal cocked his head. "Oh!" He smiled brightly. "My parents were really happy they got a weekend alone! They say they look forward to the retreat every year."

Ms. Wiggins shook her head and the bells on her headband tinkled softly. "How about you, Max? You always get a lot out of our little retreats."

Max happily took the stick from Sal. "I wrote fifteen poems in my head. *Fifteen!* My mother called my literary agent, and we're all optimistic my publisher will buy another book, even though my past sales have been less than stellar." He frowned. "Poetry is a tough market."

Ms. Wiggins smiled sympathetically. "Sales are important, but don't forget that the actual process of creation is more important than money."

Max scoffed. "Tell that to my agent."

"How about Fiona? You can surely add a fresh perspective to our retreat. What did you find out about yourself last weekend?"

Fiona nervously took the talking stick from Max. "I, uh . . ."

She looked at me, and all I could think was how hard it was going to be for her to make up a "fresh perspective" on something she hadn't spent any time at.

"Uh, I had a lot of time to think."

Darcy rolled her eyes.

"And I realized," she continued, "how important it is to try and help people. We all may be different, but we need to be there for each other." She looked at me. "And we can't give up—ever, because all creatures, great and small, are counting on us."

Tears pooled in Ms. Wiggins's eyes. "*This* is what I'm talking about, people! *This* is insight and growth. *This* is what the weekend at Peaceful Planet is all about—fostering a sense of togetherness."

Just then Raphael rushed into the room with his

backpack slung over his shoulders and his bagpipe case in hand. "Sorry I'm late!"

"Mr. Santos," Ms. Wiggins chided, "where have you been?"

"I had an extra bagpipe lesson this morning. My teacher wanted to hear my new composition. I'm hoping to use it to audition for a spot in the Thanksgiving parade. He loved it but thought I should come up with a different title. Apparently he thinks 'The Rodents of Orkney' might turn some people off their holiday dinners."

Serena pretended to gag. "'*Rodents* of Orkney?' You are seriously deranged."

Max laughed for a second and then sat up straight. He stared blankly ahead and his fingers began to twitch. "Army of rodents, music leads them with its song, mice—yours to command."

Max dissolved in a fit of laughter, joined by Sal and Serena.

"You'd be like the Pied Piper!" Nahla laughed. "You could play your bagpipes and make all of the rodents of Bridgeport do whatever you wanted."

"Children!" Ms. Wiggins snapped. "I thought we were having a serious discussion about our retreat. Why don't we move on to our election speeches?" Ms. Wiggins suggested. "We'll start with secretary and move our way up. As always, I'm hoping someone might get inspired to launch a last-minute campaign to liven up the election process." She looked hopefully around, but no one spoke up.

"Very well. Sal, you're up first."

After Sal, Raphael, and Max gave their speeches, then it was time for the presidential candidates. Ms. Wiggins clapped her hands as Max took his place back on the rug. "I'm so happy we have an actual runoff for our next electoral post. I encourage the rest of you to be inspired by Darcy and Fiona—dig deep within your souls next year and be willing to put yourself and your beliefs out there for the public vote. And never forget, losing an election does not mean you're a failure, it simply means—"

"You're unpopular," Darcy broke in.

"No! No! No!" Ms. Wiggins insisted as her head jingled with each word. "It means the current political climate does not suit your agenda, but the tide is *always* turning and you never know when the majority will side with your point of view. Now let's flip a coin to see who goes first."

Ms. Wiggins took out a sliver dollar from her pocket and tossed it in the air.

"Heads!" Darcy called out.

The coin landed in Ms. Wiggins's hand and she

looked down. "Heads it is. Darcy, we are all looking forward to hearing your point of view on the office of president and why we should vote for you."

Darcy stood up, smiling smugly. "Perhaps *Maggie* can help me get my laptop set up."

"Sure," I said.

As I joined Darcy at her desk, she narrowed her eyes. "I want to hear the spell."

"Fine." I looked at everyone sitting on the rug, talking softly. "I *wish* neither Darcy nor Fiona has an unfair advantage in the election." I turned to her. "Satisfied?"

She put her nose in the air. "Yes, now be prepared to be dazzled by your future president."

Darcy stood in front of the whiteboard and I connected her laptop to the system. The national anthem blared out of the speakers as a picture of Darcy popped up, with a flag waving in the wind at her side.

"For the last five years I have held the post of president and, until today, have run unopposed. Why? Because the rest of you know I am uniquely qualified for the job."

The next picture popped up showing a collage of Darcy holding first-place ribbons. "For the last five years I've dominated the science fair and mathletes and even taken home the gold numerous times at the Country Values Club showcase. I've had my scientific discoveries written up in journals and have remained at the top of this very class."

The next picture showed Fiona with a big, red question mark superimposed across her face. "My worthy opponent is an enigma with no track record and who, until this year, was an unsuccessful candidate for this very school."

"Darcy!" Ms. Wiggins shouted.

Darcy quickly moved to the next picture, in which her own face was now shown hovering over the White House. "In conclusion, as president I will continue to be the face of leadership for this class and will do my best to continue leading the way to perfection. Thank you."

Ms. Wiggins glared at Darcy as she sat down on the rug, and Serena high-fived her.

"Ms. Fitzgerald, it is now your turn," Ms. Wiggins said.

Fiona stood up and nervously pulled on the end of one of her braids. "Um, I don't have anything fancy planned like Darcy."

Serena and Darcy sniggered.

"But I, uh, I do think being president isn't about being the best. It's about making this classroom a place where you can follow your dreams and no will tease you about it. It's about cheering Nahla on as she tries to find the best way to make her tree grafts work. It's about Max and his haikus and encouraging him to keep writing them, even if we don't always get them. It's about thinking there's nothing strange about a bagpipe composition dedicated to mice. Most of all it's about letting people have their passions and just accepting them."

Fiona bit her lip and took a deep breath. "The most important thing is that we work together and we help each other and . . ." She looked at Darcy. "And we don't sell anyone out just to be number one." She shrugged. "The end."

Ms. Wiggins jumped up with tears in her eyes. "Well," she said with a sniffle. "It's time to fill out our ballots. We will announce the winners tomorrow at our morning meeting. To your seats, everyone."

"Hey, Raphael," Nahla said as we all stood up. "Sorry about the Pied Piper thing."

Raphael gave her a maniacal smile. "Mwa-ha-ha!" he laughed. "You'd better watch your back or I will lead my evil mice minions to attack your apple-pear hybrid tree."

Nahla rolled her eyes. "Funny. Not."

As she left shaking her head, my eyes opened wide. "The Pied Piper," I whispered. I remembered Mr. Fishbone's words: *"I'd shrink myself to the size of a mouse. That ways I could reach all the nooks and crannies a big person couldn't."*

"Raphael! Fiona! Come here!"

I pulled them into the reading nook. "What if we really

did have an army of mice we could use to search *the castle?*"

They stared at me.

"We could bewitch Raphael's bagpipes so when he plays 'The Rodents of Orkney' he attracts all of the mice on the grounds like the Pied Piper, and then we lead them to the castle to search for the sealskins. They can reach the places we never could!"

Fiona nodded her head rapidly. "It might work."

"But what kind of a spell could we use to make the mice actually do our bidding?" Raphael asked.

"Well . . . ," I started. "I haven't got it all worked out yet. But let's go to the shop after school and see if Mr. McGuire can help."

"I'll see if I can call my mom so I can go home with you," Fiona said. "I'll tell her we still need to work on that project we made up."

"Children!" Ms. Wiggins called out. "You should be at your seats."

I turned around and found Darcy standing right behind us. "Why are you always lurking around spying on us?" I hissed.

Darcy looked over her shoulders and then back at us. "I think I may be able to help. I'll meet you at the shop after school." Without saying another word she raced to her seat.

# 16

## The Rodents
## of the Orkney Islands

I opened the apartment door after school and Fiona
and Raphael followed me in. "Gram? I'm home!"

There was no reply, and then I saw a note on the
kitchen table. "She's at the food pantry. But she wrote
there's been no update about Hasenpfeffer's condition." I
shook my head. "Well, let's get the shop and see if we can
finally finish this repair job!"

I scribbled where we were going on the bottom of
Gram's note, and we headed out.

"So you've got the Pied Piper spell worked out?"
Raphael said.

I nodded. "I'm using Max's haiku and a whole bunch of magic dust number seven!"

"If only Max knew," Raphael said. "He'd be thrilled."

"Well," I continued, "I'm still not sure about getting the mice to act like bloodhounds—that's still a big question mark."

"Couldn't you just make a wish?" Fiona asked.

"I don't think so. When I was reading *Search and Rescue*, I read that it's harder to cast spells on animals than people because their brains aren't wired like ours. It's hard to magic out instinct."

We turned down Barnum Avenue, and Fiona pointed toward the shop. There was a shiny, dark car parked out front. The door opened, and Darcy stepped out. "I'll just be a minute," she said to the driver, who I couldn't see behind the tinted glass.

She held out a piece a paper as we approached. "This will get the mice to do what you want them to. After you use the spell, you need to destroy it and forget it or face the wrath of the Loyal Order of Lion Tamers—not a crew you want to mess with."

I took the paper and unfolded it. "Where did you get this?" I asked after I read the spell.

Darcy looked quickly back at the car and then leaned in close to us. "My Gammy. She used to travel around

Europe with a trained-squirrel act. She had them driving little cars and dancing to music."

Raphael burst out laughing. *"Dancing squirrels?"*

Darcy poked him in the chest. "Yes, dancing squirrels! Squirrels are incredibly hard to control, but Gammy got a spell from a lion tamer—something they usually guard very carefully and only pass on to their immediate family."

"How did she get him to give it to her?" Fiona asked. "Did she cast a spell?"

Darcy shook her head. "Gammy was quite the looker in her day, and she sweet-talked a guy into giving it to her."

"I still think dancing squirrels are funny," Raphael said as he rubbed his chest.

"Well, it won't be funny if my mother finds out I told you. My parents don't like people to know Gammy was a side-show performer, but she used to work with Sir Roderick's mother—*she* was a bearded lady. She used magic to make a beard grow, and she made a fortune doing it. But just make sure you keep your mouths shut or you're all dead meat—lion's meat to be exact."

I drew my fingers across my lips like I was zipping them shut, and Fiona did the same.

Raphael grimaced. "You won't hear a peep out of me," he mumbled through his closed lips.

"Anyway," Darcy said, "Mr. McGuire probably has most of the ingredients for the spell, but I guarantee he won't have this." She handed me a small plastic baggie filled with translucent white powder. "Moon dust—add this to the spell and the mice will fly like reindeers if you tell them to."

Fiona stared at the bag. "Moon dust—really?"

"The moon's cycles can influence animals," Darcy said. "There hasn't been a moonwalk in ages, so it's very rare."

I looked down at the bag of moon dust again. "I don't know how to thank you, Darcy. Do you want to come with us back to Scotland? I'm sure the Lachlans would appreciate you helping them."

"No, I need to get home before my mother starts asking questions. I don't want to give her a reason to poke through the pantry and find out the moon dust is missing. Oh, there's one more thing." She pulled a round watch attached to a gold chain out of her pocket. "You'll need this." She placed the watch in my hand and then opened the car door. "Step on it, Gammy!"

She slammed the door shut, and the car sped away from the curb, kicking up a cloud of dust from the street.

"Well, what are we waiting for?" Fiona asked.

We raced down the steps, and I grabbed the door handle. "It's locked. Mr. McGuire must not be here, but I have an extra key."

"She stole it last week," Raphael told Fiona.

"Borrowed!" I retorted as I sorted through my key chain.

We walked into the dark shop, and Raphael put his bagpipe case on the floor and then flipped the light switch. I placed Gammy Davenport's spell on the counter and read through the list of ingredients again. "We need poppy flowers for their hypnotic properties, corn feed, moon dust, and yeast. It says the yeast helps increase the amount of the feed depending on how many animals you're giving it to. We'll need magic dust number four, too—that binds the ingredients—and then we're good to go. Once we give the feed to the mice, we swing the watch back and forth in front of them and recite the spell. I'll mix the ingredients. Fiona, why don't you write a note to send to the Lachlans to tell them we're coming, and, Raphael, you get the mirror. It must be in the back room."

Fiona walked behind the counter and took out some writing paper and an envelope.

"Maggie," Raphael said, "the mirror isn't in there."

"Are you sure?"

He nodded. "It would be hard to miss something that big."

My stomach sank. "Where could it be?"

"Look," Fiona said. "There's a letter here from that Viola Klemp lady. Apparently she was sending some people over to collect the mirror so they could investigate getting Milo out."

My shoulders slumped. "How are we going to get to Scotland?"

Raphael shrugged. "I guess we'll have to wait until the mirror is back."

"Or you could take us, Maggie," Fiona said.

"Huh? And how am I supposed to do that?"

"Couldn't you transport us? I saw you move from one side of stage to the other at Milo's show." She held out her arm and pointed to the bracelet I'd made her. "If we're holding hands, I bet the power of the bracelets would bring us along to Scotland with you."

Raphael gaped at Fiona. "Are you insane? Maggie's never transported herself more than fifteen feet, and you trust she could take you thousands of miles? We'd probably drop into the middle of the ocean and get eaten by sharks."

"Yeah," I said. "That's not a risk I want to take."

Fiona walked around the counter and took my hand. "See if you can take me into the back room."

I stared at her. "Are you serious?"

"Try it," she said.

I squeezed her hand. "Okay, let's do it."

Raphael threw his arms into the air. "You're *both* insane," he said. "Even if you get Fiona back there in one piece, it doesn't mean you can get us to Scotland!"

"It doesn't mean I can't either." I took a deep breath as Raphael covered his eyes with his hands.

"I can't watch," he said, and then started humming loudly to himself.

I concentrated on the back room and squeezed Fiona's hand even tighter. *"I wish we were in the back room!"*

My feet were swept off the floor, and in an instant Fiona and I were in the back room.

"Ugh, I don't feel so good," Fiona said breathlessly, "but you did it!"

I leaned forward with my hands on my knees and swallowed back some bile in my throat. "Yeah, it's not the best way to travel."

"Let's try someplace farther—like the sidewalk," Fiona said.

We clasped hands, and I pictured the top of the stairs outside the shop. *"I wish we were at the top step!"*

We both laughed when we reappeared on the top step.

"This is utterly amazing!" Fiona gasped despite the greenish tinge to her face.

"Come on," I said, pointing down the stairs. "Let's tell Raphael our experiment was a success."

I opened the door and saw Raphael looking in the back room. "Maggie?" he said in a high-pitched squeak. "Fiona?" He started waving his hands at his sides. "Oh my gosh—they've disintegrated into nothingness. What am I going to—"

"We're over here," I called out.

Raphael screamed as he twisted around to face us.

"We thought we should try it one more time," Fiona said.

He put his hand to his chest. "Thanks for telling me! I thought you'd disappeared completely."

"Sorry, but let's get everything ready, and I'll take you both to the castle."

Raphael held his hands out in front of him. "This still doesn't prove you can take us to Scotland."

Fiona shook her head. "Of course it does."

"You don't have to come," I said. "I just thought you wanted to help."

He screwed up his face and turned himself in a circle. "I don't know. I do, but . . ."

"Just imagine your composition coming to life as you stand in *Scotland* playing your bagpipes."

"Uh . . ." He hung his head. "Okay. But if I die, I'm going to kill you."

I held out my hand and shook his. "You've got a deal. Now let's go!"

"Aaaaaaaaaaaaaaaaaaaaaaaaaah!" Raphael screamed in my ear as we landed in front of the castle.

He tumbled to the ground, and Fiona looked at me and shook her head. "Boys."

"That was the longest two seconds of my life." He pushed himself up and brushed grass from the knees of his pants. "Oh, great—how am going to explain grass stains to my mother?"

"Mr. McGuire said ogre lice are really good for getting out stains," I told him.

He scoffed. "I'm sure my mom has plenty of that in the laundry room."

"Just put your pipe together, and let's see if I can make these spells work."

"Look," Fiona said. "The Lachlans are coming."

I turned to see Sir Roderick—who looked like he'd aged considerably since we'd last seen him—limping alongside his wife, who held her arm out to steady him. Lyra ran ahead and greeted us.

"I can't believe this," she said. "I looked out at the lawn and saw you three pop up. I had no idea you could do that."

"Ya brought your friends back as well?" Sir Roderick asked when he finally reached us. "McGuire didn't let on ya had the power to pull off a trick like that. It's lucky these two weren't dropped in the ocean!"

Raphael's eyes popped.

"Just keep working!" I said before he could hit me with an I-told-you-so.

"We got your letter," Mrs. Lachlan said. "Do you really think you can find the pelts?"

"We're going to try," I answered.

Raphael screwed in the melody pipe and then put the bag under his arm. He put the mouthpiece between his lips and began to blow up the bag. "Okay," he said after a few minutes. "I'm ready."

"Close your eyes," I said. "Here comes a magic dust number seven shower."

Raphael squeezed his eyes shut and plugged his nose. I shook out the magic dust, and it glittered like gold in the air as it fell around him.

"Fire it up!" I said.

Raphael pressed his arm down on the bag. The pipes groaned to life. He began to move his fingers up and down the melody pipe while he kept blowing to keep the bag inflated.

I took out my wand and pointed it at Raphael. *"Army of rodents, music leads them with its song, mice—ours to command!"*

Raphael kept playing and I held my breath, praying it would work. Then I saw it. A rustling in the wind-blown grass and small, brown shapes scurrying out from between rocks and cracks in the walls.

"They're coming," Fiona whispered. "Look at all of them."

Minutes later the grass was a sea of mice all staring intently at Raphael.

"Time for phase two!" I yelled over the music. "Keep playing."

Fiona poured out handfuls of the feed we'd mixed to Mrs. Lachlan and Lyra, and they followed her lead and tossed them onto the grass.

"Please let this work," I said. I held the pocket watch and dangled it from its chain in front of the crowd of squeaking mice scrambling over one another to devour the magic feed. *Wild beasts big and small, obey my beck and heed my call, complete the task, do not fail, let only my will prevail.*

The mice stopped what they were doing and looked up. Their heads swayed back and forth, following the watch swinging like a pendulum. My heart raced as I thought this just might work. I took a deep breath and tried the spell I'd used earlier. *From sea to beach to solid ground, two worlds unite, what's lost is found; search the castle, take a peek, a selkie's skin is what you seek.*

I nodded to Raphael, who started to walk toward the castle, his bagpipes booming with music. The mice formed a writhing line behind him, and I raced ahead and opened the door.

In a flash the mice rushed past Raphael with a deafening squeak. "Can I stop now?" he asked anxiously.

"I think we're good. Let's see what these critters find."

"But . . . ," Fiona said as she ran to my side. "I don't understand. I thought they'd spread out to search the castle, but they're all heading to the tapestry room."

I shook my head as my heart sank. "I don't know what's going on."

"Follow them!" Lyra called out.

We entered the room and saw that the mice were all piled on the bearskin rug. I stamped my foot in frustration. "It's that stupid rug again," I snarled.

Sir Roderick and his wife joined us. "What's going on?" Mrs. Lachlan asked. "Did they find them?"

"No," I said, overwhelmed with disappointment. "When I tried different retrieval spells the other night the bearskin rug kept appearing. The mice somehow zeroed in on it." I hung my head. "I'm sorry. I really thought this would work."

"Wait, Maggie," Raphael said. "Do you remember the hats in Milo's basement?"

"Yeah, only they weren't really hats, they . . ." I looked at the mice climbing over the rug, and then turned to Sir Roderick. "Could you have hidden the pelts in plain sight? Could the bearskin rug really be the sealskins?"

Sir Roderick cocked his head and looked over at the rug. I watched his eyes trace over the wide-open mouth of the bear, down to its hind legs. "Yes," he whispered.

He turned and looked at me. *"Yes!"* He hobbled over to the rug and whipped out his wand. *"Go back where you came from!"* he screamed as he slashed his wand over the rug.

The mice disappeared, and Sir Roderick pulled at his beard as he limped around the rug. "What do I do? How can I right me wrong?"

Lyra walked toward him. "Father."

Sir Roderick shook his head. "I can't even look at ya, I'm so filled with shame. Can ya ever forgive yer old man for being such a selfish fool?"

Lyra put a finger under his chin and gently titled his head up. "It will be all right." She held out her hand, and Sir Roderick put his wand in it. She pointed it at the rug. "Show me what is rightfully mine!"

The mouth of the rug let out a loud roar, snapped shut, and then began to smolder. A foul rotten-egg smell filled the room, and in a flash of yellow flames the rug exploded.

"No!" I cried, thinking the skins had been destroyed. But as the smoke cleared I saw the outline of two seals on the floor.

Mrs. Lachlan rushed over and grabbed the larger one. She held it to her cheek and spun around and looked toward the ocean. Then she bent and picked up the other. "For you, my darling. This is your other half—your other life."

Lyra took the skin from her mother, and when she touched it, it grew before our eyes until it was almost as big as her mother's.

Mrs. Lachlan's lower lip trembled. "They're calling me."

"Go!" Sir Roderick cried. "Go! And tell them how sorry I am for keeping you away all these years."

Without uttering a word Mrs. Lachlan dashed from the room. I heard the front door slam open, and she was gone.

"I love you, Rhona," Sir Roderick sobbed as Lyra wrapped him in her arms.

I tilted my head toward the entryway. "We should go," I whispered to Raphael and Fiona.

They nodded, and we quietly made our way out of the room.

"I thought I'd feel happier," I said.

"Me too," Fiona said.

"Maggie," Lyra called out. "I can't let you go without thanking you."

I shrugged. "I just wanted there to be a happy ending for everyone." I looked past her into the tapestry room, where Sir Roderick was crying. "I was wrong."

Lyra gave me a hint of a smile. "Our story isn't over yet by far, but you've given us a new ending for sure."

"I hate to ask, with all this going on, but would it be possible to see Hasenpfeffer before we go?"

Lyra's eyes opened in surprise. "But he's *gone*."

My eyes welled up with tears as my body froze. "Gone?"

"Yes, gone home with Franny. He's all right, I thought you knew."

I shook my head. "I didn't! Raphael! Fiona! We have to leave now!"

# 17

## Viola Klemp

I transported us all to my room, and Hasenpfeffer shrieked when we materialized right in front of his cage. *"For pity's sake!* I almost died, and now you want to give me a heart attack!"

I opened his cage and scooped him out.

"Hey, take it easy," he complained. "Don't manhandle me while I'm still recovering!"

"I'm so glad you're back," I whispered in his ears.

I felt his body relax, and he nuzzled into my neck. "It's good to be *home*," he sighed.

Raphael cleared his throat. "I'd better be going. I

told my mom I'd be back half an hour ago."

"Yeah," Fiona said. "My mom should be here any minute to pick me up."

"Hey, guys," I said before they left, "thanks for all your help."

I put Hasenpfeffer down gently on my bed and lay down next to him. "I found the sealskins."

"I'm not surprised," he replied. "You just can't help poking your nose in other people's business. You're quite the busybody, you know."

I nodded. "I know."

Hasenpfeffer snuggled into the crook of my arm and I stroked his soft fur.

"I like the sign," he said.

"Believe it or not, Gram made it."

"I knew the old bird liked me. What's not to like after all?" He sighed. "Maggie?"

"Yes?"

"After almost dying and all, I feel I should tell you I wasn't exactly truthful before—about Milo. We did travel, and he *was* big in Japan, but I was always in a cage packed in with all the props. I was never in the fancy hotel rooms. I never got any fan mail, either."

I kept petting him and didn't say anything.

"I didn't want you to think I was a nothing," he

continued. "I thought if you believed I was a big star, you wouldn't get rid of me—like Milo did."

"I don't care if you're a star or not. You're my friend, and I'm *never* giving you up."

Hasenpfeffer sniffed. "And I don't care that you're never going to be a star on a stage because you like working in that musty old shop."

"I'm glad we understand each other," I said.

"Me too."

The next weekend I walked into the shop to see what was on the to-do list. When I got there I found the now familiar daisy-covered van parked outside and Mr. Fishbone dancing a jig in the middle of the shop.

"Money, money, money," he was singing.

"Hi," I said.

He stopped short. "Guess what? Me bill is paid in full, and I'm booked up for the next *six* months!"

Mr. McGuire came out of the back room. "Here's the werewolf saliva. I think this will help deepen your balloon dogs' barks."

Mr. Fishbone took a jar from Mr. McGuire and shook the foamy liquid around. "This will do the trick. People been complaining the dogs' barks are right annoying and giving 'em headaches."

Suddenly Mr. McGuire's mailbox started to shake and whistle. The letters LL appeared in the mist.

"It's from Lyra!" I said.

Mr. McGuire waved away the steam and took out a brown envelope. "It's addressed to you."

I opened the envelope and pulled out the letter. "Lyra *and her mother* have invited us for tea."

Mr. McGuire wiped his eyes with his bandanna. "She came back."

I nodded. "She came back!"

"Aw," Mr. Fishbone said, "ain't that wonderful."

The door to the shop swung open and a skinny woman marched in. She had tight brown curls clipped close to her head and wore a white blouse buttoned up to her chin.

Mr. Fishbone gasped. "Viola!"

I gaped at the woman. She was nothing like I had imagined. I'd thought she'd be a grandmotherly type with gray hair and soft eyes, trying to clean up the world of magic. In reality, Viola Klemp was a hard, birdlike woman with a sharp, hooked nose and frown lines marking her face.

Viola looked around the shop, breathed deep, and locked her dark eyes on mine. "Maggie Malloy?"

"Yes?" I quivered.

"I'm here to deliver your license." She took an envelope out of a small purse. "From what I understand you successfully completed a test on the ethical use of magic and underwent a series of trials to determine the scope of your abilities."

I looked at Mr. McGuire. I hadn't done any of that, and I wasn't sure what to say.

"She passed her tests with flying colors," he said.

"Yes," I said quietly.

Viola nodded curtly and gave me the envelope. "Very well, then, you are now known to the magic world as a level-fifty magician."

Mr. Fishbone gaped at me. "That's quite the number, missy."

Viola glared at him. "Yes, it is. And as such, know that I will be keeping an eye on you. Magicians at this level often get full of ideas about how to use their magic— ideas the Society of Ethical Magicians do not condone."

I shook my head. "I won't get any ideas. None at all."

She looked down her nose at me. "We shall see. Despite what you may have heard, we society members take our job very seriously and will not tolerate magicians who think they are above our guidelines." She turned on a heel of her pointed shoes and stalked over to Mr. Fishbone. "Clarence. I hear you've upgraded your act."

He paled. "Who, who said that?" he asked nervously.

"Word gets around," she said, and then gave him a cold smile. "But I know you wouldn't do anything to jeopardize the veil of secrecy the society recommends we use to keep our activities under the radar."

Mr. Fishbone trembled. "No. No I wouldn't." He gulped. "You can count on me!"

She narrowed her eyes. "Good." She looked up and regarded Mr. McGuire. "I have no news to report about Milo, but we should be concluding our tests on the mirror shortly, and then we'll have it promptly returned. I trust you will continue to use it with the utmost caution."

Mr. McGuire snapped is suspenders. "Absolutely," he said.

"Very good, I have other business to attend to, so I will be off. It was good to meet you, Maggie. Hopefully I shan't be receiving any more reports citing acts of misconduct."

I nodded, and then Viola Klemp tucked her small black purse under her arm and strutted out of the shop.

Mr. Fishbone whistled. "She's a tough old bird, she is. I thought getting dismissed by the chairman of the Federation of Magic woulda taken her down a notch. If anything it's made her meaner. I best be going too. I think I need to work on me act some more."

"Good luck with that, Clarence," Mr. McGuire said.

Mr. Fishbone put the werewolf saliva in his suitcase and left the shop muttering about Viola Klemp.

"Well, let's see that license," Mr. McGuire said.

I smiled as I ripped the envelope open. I took out a small plastic card with my name and picture on it. "Level fifty." I gave the card to Mr. McGuire and noticed there was a paper inside the envelope. "Hey, there's a note—it's from Sir Roderick. It says, 'Dear Maggie. I thought it best to put you no higher than a level fifty. There are many reasons it's prudent not to advertise the level of an extremely powerful magician. While I do not know the true extent of your power, nor do I care to, you successfully retrieved the sealskins, thus breaking an irretrievable spell. In order to perform such a feat, you would have to be at a level *one hundred*. My family and I are looking forward to having you to the castle again soon. Sincerely, Sir Roderick.'"

I looked up at Mr. McGuire. "It's a good thing Viola Klemp didn't see this!"

He took the note from my hand. "Yes, and I think it would be wise to destroy it before anyone else sees it." He put the note on the counter and pointed his wand at it. "Fire!" he said. An orange flame shot out of the tip and ignited the paper. It burned quickly until just a few bits of ash remained.

He turned to me. "Well, level one hundred. That will come in handy for future repair jobs. Speaking of which, we have a cauldron being delivered soon. You did such a good job repairing the last one with cauldron burps that I just may put my feet up and let you do all the work."

I groaned. "I'll get the apron and boots from the bathroom."

"Will Fiona or Raphael be joining us today?"

I shook my head. "Raphael is at his cousin's and Fiona is spending the day at Darcy's. Fiona is our new class president—by a unanimous vote."

Mr. McGuire raised an eyebrow in surprise.

"I know. We couldn't believe Darcy didn't vote for herself either. I think she was feeling guilty about what happened in Scotland, but you could tell she regretted it almost immediately. After Fiona made her acceptance speech telling us all the things she was wanted to accomplish as president, Darcy cornered her and insisted on being her chief adviser and said they'd meet at her house to discuss her 'misguided ideas.'"

Mr. McGuire clucked his tongue. "Well, it's just us today, then. I'm going to do some paperwork while you prep for the cauldron."

I headed into the bathroom, where I got the rubber gloves and apron from under the sink. When I stood up

I thought I saw a flash of something red in the bathroom mirror. I stared at my reflection as my heart raced. Red was Milo the Magnificent's favorite color.

"That's the way," a voice whispered. "I knew you could do it. You rub my back, and I'll rub yours."

Goose bumps broke out on my arms. The voice wasn't Milo's; it was old and creaky-sounding, with a faint accent. I looked all around the bathroom and then stood still listening for more.

"We'll get her soon," the voice whispered. *"Very soon."*